A Town
Called
Fury

A Town Called Fury

William W. Johnstone

and

J. A. Johnstone

PINNACLE BOOKS
Kensington Publishing Corp.
www.kensingtonbooks.com

PINNACLE BOOKS are published by

Kensington Publishing Corp.
850 Third Avenue
New York, NY 10022

ISBN 0-7860-1741-4

First printing: July 2006

10 9 8 7 6 5 4 3 2 1

Printed in the United States of America

1

Kansas City, Missouri, 1865

Jedediah Fury put down his paintbrush and bucket of whitewash, struck a match on the sole of his dusty boot, then set it to his pipe. Puffing in the sweet smoke, he sat down on a bale of straw and looked out over his future; more like, what his future had been reduced to.

He saw a house in town, small compared to the one he'd left behind back East, but still neat and tidy; three good saddle geldings, enclosed by the corral fence he'd just finished whitewashing half of; a milk cow in the tiny barn that had come with the place; a handful of clucking, pecking hens; a few newly purchased stoats, presently rooting and quarreling in their pen; and his old short-bed Conestoga wagon, the one that had made so many trips from the East Coast to the Western Shore and back again.

He really ought to figure out just how many miles he'd put under those wheels, he thought.

Or maybe not. He wasn't exactly sure he wanted to know how much time—how much blood, sweat, tears, and effort—he'd put into guiding pilgrims into the wilderness over the past twenty years. Well, not much the last few. Of course, people had wanted to go west, be shown the way, but he'd been more than a little preoccupied with the War. He'd given it his heart and his soul, not to mention two sons and a wife.

His only remaining boy, Jason, had almost caught up with him on the other side of the fence. Jason made the last few strokes with the paintbrush and then carefully opened the gate and let himself out, placing his brush and paint bucket alongside his father's. He didn't join his father, however. He went to the pump and began to wash his hands.

"Nice job, son," Jedediah said around his pipe.

"Yeah," Jason replied without looking up. "Looks good." He paused and took a long look down the fence. "Your side, too, Pa," he added, a bit grudgingly.

Jedediah chuckled softly. Everything was grudging with that boy. Although he reminded himself that Jason wasn't a boy any longer. Twenty wasn't a boy, was it? No, at twenty, Jedediah himself had been trapping beaver and wolf in the Colorado Territory with Wash Keough, fighting off grizzlies and the frigid weather and the temptation to take a squaw to wife. He had managed to win out over all of them.

Jedediah sighed. No, twenty was no boy.

"Jason, after you finish up there, could you hike over to the mercantile and pick up a few pounds of flour for your sister?" He relit his pipe, which had gone out.

Finally, Jason twisted his head around. He'd just splashed his face with water, and it was dripping. Jason's mother, Jane, had always said that Jeremy had all the enthusiasm of the three, Jonathon had all the sweetness, and Jason had the good looks that would lead him either to prison or the U.S. Senate.

She'd been right, Jedediah figured. Jeremy, their eldest, had been so damned eager to please his senior officer that he'd led his squadron on a suicide mission into the swamps of Georgia and had died right along with the rest of them, probably to the shrieks and cackles of Rebel yells. Jedediah figured that if Jason had been in his older brother's position, he would have told his commanding officer to take a long walk off a short pier.

As for his youngest, Jonathon, well, the boy had been too kindhearted for his own good, God bless him. One afternoon, he'd invited a party of travelers to come in for some of his Ma's good cooking. Which was nothing that he hadn't seen his pa do countless times before.

But what Jonathon didn't know that day was that the very fellows he'd invited into the parlor were the same four that had, not three hours before, held up a bank down in Maryland and shot two men. They killed the boy and his mother before leaving the house. Little Jenny survived, but only because she had the sense to run and hide out back, in the woods.

"Flour? What for?"

Jedediah was jerked back into the present. "Your sister's making dinner."

A look of long-suffering martyrdom spread over the boy's face. "Aw, Pa! Why'd you want to go and let her cook again? Last time—"

Jedediah cut his son off with a wave of his hand. "We all have our unfortunate accidents, Jason. Don't go mentioning it in front of Jenny."

"Why not?"

"It hurts her feelings," Jedediah said, while throwing one of his *you-know-better-than-to-ask-that* looks.

It was wasted, though. Jason wasn't paying him any mind. His eyes were focused up toward the street, instead.

Jedediah followed his son's gaze to a small contingent of people marching up the graveled driveway. Could this mean a new trip to the wild country? He stood up and walked forward.

"Afternoon, folks!" he announced, in a voice that he hoped was authoritative, yet benign. "The Good Father" was the face he liked people to see, particularly people he was going to have to ferry across the wilderness.

"Don't get started yet," he heard Jason softly say behind him. "They might only be trying to get us to join the Baptist church."

And Jedediah thought, *No, by God, twenty isn't yet a man, not when it's that flip and sarcastic. . . .*

The tall man at the front of the group came right up to him and stuck out his hand, taking Jedediah's and pumping it vigorously. "Mr. Fury, sir?" When Jedediah nodded in the affirmative, the man continued. "I'm the Reverend Milcher, Louis Milcher, that is, and this is my wife, Lavinia." The small, tired-looking woman next to Milcher curtsied timidly.

"Reverend," replied Jedediah with a nod. "Ma'am. Pleased to make your acquaintance." Jason had been right after all: They were trolling for new congregational members. Even though he was pretty certain he knew what was coming, he asked, "What can I do for you folks?"

"I have been voted spokesman for our group, Mr. Fury," Milcher went on. "We are only eight wagons and a small gather of livestock, but I am certain that we can attract a few more fellow pilgrims when it's known that we have procured the great Jedediah Fury as our wagon master!"

Surprised yet not surprised, Jedediah scratched at his chin. "Where you folks planning on ending up?" By the looks of them, they'd be lucky to make it across the Missouri River into Kansas.

"Why, California, sir!" said Milcher, as if everybody in the world could have only one possible destination.

"Whereabouts in California?"

"I plan to go to southern California," confided Milcher. "I have already purchased land there, in a place outside the town of Los Angeles. Have you heard of it?"

Jedediah had heard of it lots of times and been there

a few, and frankly, he couldn't see why anybody outside of a rattler or a family of scorpions would want to live there.

But he asked, "Why don't you folks step on into the house?" and gestured toward the back porch. Over his shoulder, he called, "You go run that errand for your sister, Jason."

He heard Jason snort, but refrained from adding a word of castigation when the boy came immediately into sight, walking up the drive toward the street.

A few of the ladies actually gasped.

"Oh, my!" commented Mrs. Milcher, one hand to her rapidly coloring cheek. "What a handsome young man!"

"Thank you," said Jedediah as he led the party up the back steps, through the enclosed porch, and into the house. Since the age of fifteen, Jason had always had the same effect on females, whether he paid them any mind or not.

The Reverend Mr. Milcher had best reel his wife in— and fast—or this trip wouldn't be smooth *or* pleasant.

Jedediah swung open the door that led to the back hall and ushered the party inside, saying, "I reckon he's a good enough boy."

Try though he might, though, he couldn't keep some pride from seeping into his voice.

Jason walked the four blocks down into the beginning of the business district, and headed for the nearest dry-goods store. He wasn't any too fond of Missouri. Or Kansas City, for that matter. If he'd had his druthers, he'd have stayed back East and gone to college, the way his folks had always promised him he would.

But the War hadn't been their fault, after all—although he would have liked very much to blame them, or, at least, his father—and there was no money. Even the sale of their old family property had barely paid off their debts. He supposed he should be grateful that his father had an established trade of sorts to fall back on.

But Jason wasn't very grateful. All he could think of was those ivied halls that he'd never see, and the only thing he could feel was cheated and envious and hurt.

As he made his way along the street, he heard someone shout from down an alley, at his left. He stopped and looked, and there in the shadows, saw a fistfight in progress. One of the fellows in it was quite a bit smaller, and was suffering the brunt of it.

Never one to just mind his own business—as his father was fond of reminding him—Jason stepped into the alley's mouth and called to the punisher, "Hey, there, you! Let him go!"

The bigger fellow, one hand on the smaller's collar, turned his head toward Jason. And smiled.

It was a very unwholesome smile.

"Get lost," he snarled, and slugged the smaller boy again. Neither of them was past twenty-one. The boy getting the worst of it seemed quite a bit younger.

The smaller boy lost consciousness and slipped to the ground. Still smiling, the victor turned to face Jason. "And just what business is it of yours, Mr. Fancy Pants?"

Don't let him tick you off, Jason told himself, but he felt himself pulling up and standing taller, all his muscles tensed and braced for the onslaught.

"Get out," Jason said. The boy on the ground was still breathing, at least. And conscious again. Jason added, "Go on home."

The bully's head—now outfitted with a scowl—twisted to the side, and he said, "Just who the hell do you think you are, anyhow?"

"I'm someone who doesn't like to see murder committed for no reason but sport."

The bully appeared taken aback and said nothing for a moment, giving Jason the time to notice the initials M.M. embroidered on one point of his collar, and that he also wore not one gun, which Jason had seen from the first, but two.

"Go on," Jason said in a voice he hoped was calm and self-assured. "Don't be stupid."

But it appeared that the fellow wasn't falling for it. Or perhaps, didn't notice. He shouted, "Stupid? Why, I'll—" as he suddenly ran toward Jason.

Jason sidestepped him at the last moment, and the bully's momentum took him out into the street and right into a mud puddle, which he promptly slipped and fell into. While he was cursing and picking himself up, Jason went to his victim and helped him to his feet.

The smaller boy stuttered, "Th-thank you. Be careful. That's Matt MacDonald!"

He said it, Jason thought, like everybody should know that name and be afraid at its mention.

Well, he wasn't.

And the bully was bearing down on him again, although he was slightly impeded by the mud soaking his pants and shirt, and the fact that he'd stepped into a bucket and it was stuck on one foot. He'd also lost one gun.

His first wild swing caught Jason square in the chest and sent him tumbling backward, into a stack of crates. But Jason rolled and came up on his feet fast, confusing the bully—who was undoubtedly accustomed to weaker and smaller opponents—and clipped him in the side of the head. The clip was followed by a sharp uppercut that laid the bully out flat—with his foot still stuck in that bucket.

"Gosh," muttered the smaller boy, who had fled behind the rain barrel.

Jason successfully fought the urge to laugh. "Duck your head in that water," Jason said to him. "You've got blood on your face. You don't want to scare your folks."

The boy obeyed, and when he and Jason walked out of the alley, leaving a cowed Matt MacDonald behind, Jason said, "What's your name, kid?"

The boy scrubbed water and blood from his face with a sleeve. "Milcher. Thomas Milcher. And I'm not a kid," he added, rather proudly. "I'm fifteen."

Jason smiled. "Sorry. Your papa a reverend?"

Thomas's hands automatically balled into defensive fists. "Yeah, what about it?"

"Stick close, then. I've gotta pick up something, then I'm going home. Your folks are there." He headed up the street again in search of a dry-goods store with young Thomas Milcher, a new acolyte, tagging at his heels.

2

Jedediah was satisfied with the group clustered about his big dining room table and packed into the corners of the room. Seven couples in all, they were a good start on a wagon train. The Reverend Milcher had done most of the talking, but Jedediah had been able to pick up a few things about the others.

Hamish MacDonald was looking to become a rancher. At least he had announced, at least three times, that he had a dozen cows, with calves at their sides, and a prime Hereford bullock and four nice Morgan mares, and was looking for land: He didn't care where, so long as there was good grazing. MacDonald, a widower, also had a boy, twenty, and a girl, sixteen.

Young Randall Nordstrom had no children, but his wife, Miranda, was a seamstress, and he had a wagonload of foodstuffs and yard goods and geegaws. They were planning on opening a store, with Miranda doing sewing and giving music lessons on the side.

There were two Morton families. Well, three. Ezekial and his wife, Eliza, had two grown daughters who were also traveling with them. Electa was single and twenty-seven. Europa was thirty, and was now Mrs. Milton Griggs—and Milton was a blacksmith and a wheelwright. They used up two wagons between them.

The other part of the Morton family was elderly Zachary Morton, a gunsmith, and his wife, Suzannah.

They had no children, at least with them, and Jedediah had at first thought that they were too old to make the trip. However, the Reverend Milcher had managed to convince him otherwise. And Zachary looked fit for his age. He sat at the far end of the table, glowering from beneath his gray and beetling brows while he fiddled with his pipe.

Next came Salmon Kendall and his wife, Cordelia. They hailed from Massachusetts, and were farmers. While Salmon had no special skills or merchandise upon which the train could count, he looked to have a strong back and a solid purpose. They had two children: Salmon Jr., called Sammy, twelve, and Peony, called for some inexplicable reason Piny, aged ten.

The Milchers themselves, he supposed, offered spiritual aid. The reverend and his wife, Lavinia, had seven kids ranging from five to fifteen. The wife seemed to have a bit of a harpy's tongue, but he supposed all those children would keep her busy. At least, he hoped so.

Altogether, the five families (counting all the Mortons as one) accounted for eight long- and short-bed Conestoga wagons; nine saddle horses and four breeding stock; a couple dozen cattle, assorted hogs, goats, two dogs, and a cat named Chuckles, which belonged to the Milchers.

It was a fine start.

"Well?" said the Reverend Milcher.

"Six or eight additional wagons, anyway," replied Jedediah thoughtfully. He really wanted at least twenty in the group. To take fewer could be foolhardy. They had plenty of hostile territory to traverse.

Eliza Morton looked crestfallen. "Where on earth can we find as many as we already are, Ezekial?"

Ezekial put an arm around his wife, comforting her. "I shouldn't think it will be too difficult, Eliza," he muttered. "After all, ain't Kansas City the great jumpin'-off place, darlin'?"

* * *

Over the next few weeks, the wagon train grew and grew. Jedediah found a group of six wagons to join up, and the Reverend Milcher found two, then five, then seven. Milcher's were mostly farmers, but within the ranks of Jedediah's recruits were some folks he considered quite useful.

Michael Morelli was a country doctor. Well, not the go-to-school kind, but he was close enough. He, his wife Olympia, and their young son Constantine and younger daughter Helen would journey complete with a traveling surgery—something that Jedediah knew, from hard experience, would come in handy.

In addition, he picked up Saul and Rachael Cohen, and their boys David, Jacob, and Abraham. The Cohens were Jews and he expected some trouble from the Reverend Milcher along the line, but he figured he'd put up with it. The Cohens planned to open a store once they got to California, and brought two wagons to the mix, one of which would be filled to the brim with stock for their new mercantile.

True, the Nordstroms were well stocked, too, but most of their stuff was yard goods and notions and the like, while the Cohens carried hardware and hand tools. If forced to choose, Jedediah would have rather had the Cohens along any day of the week.

The rest of his recruits were farmers or potential ranchers, although Seth Wheeler had done some smithing in his time, or so he said.

The best he could say for Milcher's new folks was that one of the women had been a nurse during the War.

But still, he was glad for the bodies and the wagons. He thought they had enough, now.

Arrangements were made, money changed hands, wagons were packed and repacked and loaded, and spirits were high. Always best to start off that way, Jedediah thought. The reality of the trip would take the wind out of their sails, but at least they were inflated with bright and airy hopes to start with.

That way, they had a lot farther to fall before they hit bottom.

As for himself, well, Jason was going with him, and Jenny was staying behind with Tom and Sally Norton, their neighbors, until he got back next year. Jedediah had arranged it all.

But Jenny wasn't having it, drat her. Right this minute, she stood before him in the front hall, her arms crossed over her chest—just like her mama—and a frown on her face.

"But I want to come!" she said for probably the fourth time. "I *am* coming!"

Jedediah let out a long sigh. "Jenny, I'll have no more of this. I told you, you're only fifteen and it's a long, hard trip."

"I know how old I am, Papa, and I know it's hard. But the boys got to go when they were only twelve!"

Jedediah opened his mouth, but she jumped back in right away.

"And don't say that they were boys!" she finished.

"Honey," Jedediah began in a measured tone, "they *were* boys. It makes a difference. You're just a young thing, learning to cook and bake and sew like your mama. Someday, you'll want to keep house for your man, and you'll want to keep it in a civilized place, not out on the wild prairie. Boys don't grow on trees out there."

She took a deep breath and looked up at him through lush, golden lashes, a glower on her pretty face. When her mama had worn that look, Jedediah knew that he was in trouble.

"Papa, I'll be safe. After all, you and Jason will be

there. Why, I could get shot by a bandit or kidnapped into a house of degradation right here in Kansas City!"

She smiled a tad when she said that last bit. Her mama would have, too.

He shook his head. "What about school?" he asked, even though he knew full well that Electa Morton intended to teach school on the trip west. He just hoped that Jenny didn't remember it.

But she did.

"Oh, radishes, Papa! I spoke with Miss Morton, and she says I can help her. I've already got my eighth-grade certification, as if you didn't know."

She had been at him so much lately that he knew he was beaten. Or would be, very shortly.

He gave in to gravity.

"All right, Jenny," he said, shaking his head. "You wore me down." She squealed and literally gave a leap up into the air while he added, "You can go along, I reckon, but you'll have to do your share, just like anybody else. You'll walk behind the wagon, do the cooking, and help with the livestock. You'll have to learn to reload in case there's trouble, you know."

"I'd rather you taught me how to shoot."

He slapped his hat on his head. "Don't press your luck, daughter," he said, and walked around her, to the front door.

Jedediah rode the half mile down to the Reverend Milcher's current place of residence—the double lot behind Barker's laundry—on his old blue roan saddle horse, Gumption. Milcher and several of his group had set up temporary camp there, and Barker was charging them a pretty penny for the pleasure.

Milcher saw him coming, and lifted a hand.

"Hail, Brother Fury!" he cried.

The greeting annoyed Jedediah a bit, but he didn't let it show on his face. "Morning, Milcher," he called. "How are you folks coming along? Ready to go in the morning?"

As Fury dismounted, Milcher walked out to meet him. "Indeed, indeed," the reverend said, nodding his head. 'We could leave this evening, if you desire."

"Tomorrow will be soon enough."

Jedediah cast a gaze toward the corral, where there stood a number of milk cows, horses, oxen, and goats. He noticed the absence of Hamish MacDonald's livestock, though, and mentioned it.

"Oh, he's moved them out to graze. Somewhere north of town." Milcher sniffed, as if he didn't approve of such consideration being paid to one's livestock. "They'll be back in time, though." He checked his watch. "I hope."

"Those cows of yours could use a little grass," Jedediah said softly. They were fair ribby and dull-eyed. "They'll get some starting tomorrow, though."

"My opinion exactly!" Milcher said, loud enough that a woman walking down the opposite side of the road heard him and stopped to stare.

Jedediah ignored Milcher's overeagerness and asked, "Where's Jason? I don't see him." Indeed, all he saw were people packing wagons and fiddling with livestock, and children playing in the spaces between the wagons.

"He went to load the water barrel wagon. He and Matt MacDonald. And Milton Griggs." Milcher pointed down the street.

Matt MacDonald? Ever since the day that Milcher had showed up on the Fury doorstep, Jason and Matt had been avoiding each other like a case of the small-pox. He hoped they were mending their fences.

"Well, then," Jedediah said, just as he noticed a stack of crates sitting beside Milcher's wagon. "Let me help with those crates, Milcher."

"Be obliged, Brother Fury."

Jedediah wouldn't stay long, though. He had his own Conestoga to pack yet again, now that Jenny was going along on the trek.

Dad blast it, anyway!

3

Jason sat his mare on the far bank of the Missouri, mopping his brow. Who would have thought it would take this long to get them all across? But only two of the ferries were operational, the cattle had decided to go downstream a mile before crossing all the way over, and the Milchers' cat had developed a sudden urge to go swimming.

He thought one of their kids had likely tossed the cat over the side, but he kept his peace and fished the poor thing out of the drink. He'd like to get his hands on that kid, though.

The cattle had been brought back upstream by his father's three hired men—Milt Billings, who Jason was surprised his father had hired, because Jason didn't trust him any farther than he could throw him; Gil Collins, who at twenty-four was the youngest of the three, and something of a cipher; and Ward Wanamaker. Jason liked Ward. He was good with livestock, good with people, and seemed to be looking forward to the journey.

The men were holding the cattle in a tight group about a hundred yards from where Jason sat his palomino, watching the final wagon roll off the ferry. Later on, the three would serve as jacks-of-all-trades, everything from Indian fighters to roustabouts to baby-walkers.

Farther out ahead, his father was lining up the rest of the wagons, making sure everybody had made it across the river high and dry. Jason doubted the Milchers' cat was faring as well as the rest of the Milchers.

He looked for Jenny, too, and spied her, the third wagon from the front, high on the driver's bench of the family Conestoga. He couldn't help but quirk his mouth up into a smile. He'd bet she hadn't figured on driving a six-in-hand when she'd begged her way into this.

Well, she'd be walking soon enough. His father had brought along extra trade goods this time, and all those mirrors and blankets and geegaws weighed as much as two fat steers, and that was in addition to their personal things. He'd also brought extra ammunition in a wagon currently driven by Tommy Milcher, and another filled with extra water for the livestock. Ward Wanamaker had left the livestock and was presently taking the ferry back to drive it over. Jenny'd have to get out and lead their team sooner or later. His father would insist.

On the road west, horses and oxen were more important than people. Unless you were starving to death.

And even then, it was iffy.

He'd noticed that the Reverend Milcher, in addition to all those kids, had brought along a piano. Probably to accompany all the hymns he'd be leading in that new church he planned to build. Jason figured that piano would probably end up somewhere beside the trail about halfway into the Indian Territory. As would the Nordstroms' big old breakfront, and Milton Griggs's anvil.

People brought the craziest things along.

He heard his father's familiar whistle, and reined his horse around, while taking a last, longing look at the eastern horizon. Good-bye to college, good fellowship, and good things. Hello tumbleweeds and wild country and sudden death.

Well, his path was set now, in the hot, dry caliche and baking sun of the land to come. He'd just have to live with it.

He gave the men a friendly wave to move up the herd, then goosed his horse into a slow lope and caught up with the plodding wagons up front.

Ten miles from the Missouri, and Lavinia was already having second thoughts about that piano. Louis had purchased it, secondhand, in Missouri, and it had seemed like a good idea at the time. Music to bring the godless back to the fold, silky songs of praise to unite the congregation into one big family.

But it weighed too much. It took up the room where three of their children could have slept, and Lavinia had left behind one hundred pounds of flour and another fifty of cornmeal to make room.

She was happy to defer to her lord and master, but not when he was being an idiot. And only an idiot would cast her children outside, to sleep beneath the wagon with the snakes. It was bad enough that they had to walk behind or alongside the wagon, that they'd have to stay there for what—fifteen hundred miles? Two thousand? They had been mad to give in to Louis's wanderlust, mad to leave their comfortable farm and their rightful place in society.

Louis had insisted there was more, though. Greener pastures, he'd said. If only his greener pastures weren't so very far away!

And now here she was, only ten miles into the wilderness, with stinging feet and throbbing thighs and aching calves and ankles swollen like the fabled elephants. Her head hurt, her eyes burned, and she could only imagine what her children were feeling.

At least Seth, at twelve, had been deemed mature

enough and lightweight enough to do the driving. Her littlest, Hope, rode beside him on the bench, and her next-to-youngest, Charity, clung to her hand and bravely tried to keep up, although Lavinia carried her half the time.

Young Thomas drove one of the communal wagons for Mr. Fury, but the rest of the children walked.

She felt a rivulet of sweat make its way down her back, underneath the stays of her corset. Perhaps Suzannah Morton had been right. This was no place for the niceties of society.

And it was no place for these shoes. The blisters rising on her heels, she stopped, putting Charity on the ground beside her. Charity didn't understand, and held up her arms with a pleading look.

Lavinia shook her head. "Mother's feet are sore, darling. She can't carry you any longer until they're bandaged. Run and ask your brother to let you ride on the wagon with Hope."

The little girl's pretty face lit up. "Yes, Mother," she said, and scampered off ahead.

Lavinia stood exactly where she had stopped for some time, letting wagon after wagon pass her, group after group of walking women and children, until the Morellis' wagon came into view. She didn't know the Morellis very well, since they were Catholic and her husband frowned on papists, but she knew that he was a doctor, and that was what she needed.

She waved at him, up there in the driver's seat, and called out, "Dr. Morelli? Dr. Morelli, I have a medical problem!"

He slowed the wagon, then pulled out of line and stopped completely. "Mrs. Milcher?" he asked, cocking a brow. He slid down to the ground and approached her. "What seems to be the problem?"

Suddenly, she was embarrassed. What if her husband

should find out she'd gone to a papist for help? He'd be angry sure enough, but still, she didn't feel she could walk another step without some sort of aid.

"My feet," she said, pointing to the ground.

He slipped an arm around her and helped her hobble to his wagon. "Those are no shoes for walking, Mrs. Milcher," he muttered. "Does one of your boys have a spare pair of boots?"

Horrified at the suggestion, she gulped and said, "Boots?"

"Yes, good, sturdy, roomy boots." Dr. Morelli was already at work with the button hook. What he produced when he pulled off her shoe shocked her. She had thought she was blistered only on her heels, for they hurt the worst, but instead, her foot was a mass of blisters, bruises, and contusions.

Morelli clucked as he removed the other shoe. He looked up and gave her a stern frown. "Women," he said. "You lame yourself for fashion."

Then he handed over her shoes and got to work with antiseptic and bandages. When he was finished, he lifted her up onto the wagon's tailgate and said, "Stay put, you hear? I don't want you on your feet for at least two days. I'll drive you up to your own rig."

Cowed and embarrassed, Lavinia Milcher simply nodded.

When they circled the wagons late that afternoon, Lavinia Milcher wasn't the only walking wounded. Three other women and girls had so damaged their feet that they'd have to ride for the next few days. Young Jacob Cohen had made the mistake of trying to play with the Milcher kids, and had taken a beating for his trouble to their gleeful cries of "Jew boy! Jew boy! Jew boy!"

Jason, torn between drowning the lot of the Milcher kids or just poleaxing their father, had settled for hollering at them, then hoisting the battered and weeping eight-year-old Jacob up into his saddle and taking him to his mother.

Fortunately, they were traveling right in front of Doc Morelli's wagon, and Mrs. Cohen whisked the boy back to the doctor before Jason had a chance to apologize for those idiot Milchers. She abandoned her wagon entirely, and Jason had to take over the driving for about a half hour.

He honestly didn't know how anybody could take sitting on those damned seats all day! By the time she got back, with a bandaged Jacob in tow, Jason's backside had bruises on its bruises. He was glad to turn the rig over and get back up on Cleo again. After that torturous ride, the palomino's smooth gait seemed like heaven.

By the time everybody was in place and the wagons were circled for the night, the sun had slipped beneath the horizon. Men turned to stripping the harness off their horses and oxen, and the woman started to fix dinner. Jason had a few words with his father, telling him of the Cohen/Milcher battle.

Jedediah simply nodded and said, "Figured it'd happen. Just didn't figure so soon." He placed a hand on Jason's shoulder. "You did the right thing, Jason. I'll take care of it. Don't know why these folks can't just get along for as long as it takes to make the goldurn trip!"

The livestock was put up, dinner was prepared, a fire had been built in the center of the circled wagons, and most folks sat round it, plates in their weary hands. Jedediah stood up slowly, dreading his speech.

He walked over to the fire, and said, "Folks? Can I have your attention?"

Gradually, the buzz of conversation died away, and all eyes were on him.

"Just wanted to say a few things," Jedediah began. "First off, you all did real well for a first day on the trail. We made twelve miles, by my reckoning."

Scattered applause broke out around the fire.

"Of course," he added, "that was all on the flat. We won't do as well later on. But by the same token, some days we'll do better. Now, most of you know that I hired us some help for the drive. Milt Billings—stand up there, Milt—is an ace horseman. He speaks Piute, Comanche, Crow, and Apache. And that's gonna come in mighty handy."

Some of the woman began to whisper nervously, but Jedediah put the kibosh on that directly, saying, "We're gonna need to trade with the natives, and that takes communication, folks."

The whispering stopped.

"Next, there's Ward Wanamaker and Gil Collins. Ward, doff your hat so's they can tell who's who."

Ward did, and smiled wide. Gil just stood there, twitching nervously.

"Ward and Gil are both as good with their guns as they are with livestock or a shovel. You get into a bind and need somebody to help with your livestock, or you need a spare driver for a spell, you call on Ward or Gil. Sit down, boys."

He paused a moment. "Now, there's something else that's been preying on my mind. Folks, we have all throwed in together in order to make this difficult trip across the wilderness. And that means leavin' our petty bigotries behind us. We've got somebody from practically everywhere in the world in our group. Folks from the north, and folks from the south, folks from the old country and the new; Protestants, Catholics, and Jews. Now, I heard about some trouble breaking out today, which is pretty damned soon for trouble. You parents, you school your young'uns to be more tolerant, else you're going to be in for a world of hurt. Everybody got that?"

The group was shocked into silence—which he'd hoped would be their reaction—and Jedediah made his way back to his place and sat down, between Jason and Jenny. "Good dinner, honey," he said, and forced down another bite of Jenny's overdone rabbit.

4

Jenny started the next day as she had started the day before. After she got herself ready, she piled every blanket and quilt she owned on the driver's bench, then waited while her papa and Jason hitched the team. It was beyond her how those other drivers made do without padding.

Jason must have seen her padding her perch, because he actually smiled at her—something he didn't do very often—and said, "Smart girl."

It was enough to plaster a smile on her face for the next two hours.

By that time, they had made another four or five miles, and her papa had ridden down the line, saying that there was a town about six miles up the trail. Jenny knew that could mean only one thing—they'd camp outside it, and some of them would be able to go in and visit. Or buy things!

Megan MacDonald, who was fast becoming her best friend, had told her there'd be gooseberries ahead, or so she thought, and ever since, Jenny had been set on getting hold of some canning jars and paraffin. The Nordstroms had some in their spare wagon, but the cost was too dear.

Well, she'd show them. She'd slip into town and get her own.

The trip, meanwhile, was baking hot. She was glad she'd worn her bonnet. It kept the sun off her face, anyway, but she knew her hands were turning brown as walnuts. Papa had given her driving gloves, but the reins were so soft and old that she hadn't needed them. Until now. She began to dig through her bag.

"Hello!" called a familiar voice.

Jenny smiled and turned to spy Megan, walking up alongside the wagon.

"Hello, yourself. Want a ride?"

Megan's pretty brows knitted. "You sure? I mean, that it's not too much load?"

"Don't be silly. Besides, I need to find my driving gloves."

"Okay," Megan chirped, and placing her foot on the step, swung up into the seat beside Jenny, who handed her the reins. "You're not blistering," Megan remarked.

"No, but my hands'll be as dark as a red Indian pretty soon."

Megan laughed. Although Jenny was two years Megan's junior, the two had hit it off right away. Megan was nothing like her overbearing father or her bully of a brother, Jenny had decided within three minutes of their first meeting. She had all the humor in the family, and a cleverness to match it. And besides, both girls had lost their mothers at an early age.

They were fast becoming sisters in spirit.

And Jenny had seen Jason watching Megan. Not overtly—that wasn't Jason's style—but just in quick glances. He appeared to like what he saw, and Jenny was glad. Perhaps, if she was lucky and said her prayers faithfully, Megan could become her sister in more than spirit.

She hadn't broached the subject to Megan, though. That would have been bad luck.

"Like what you've done to the seat," Megan said, as Jenny pulled on the first glove. They were men's gloves and she swam in them.

Jenny laughed. "Don't know why everybody didn't think of it."

"Oh, they will before too long," Megan said. "If you know what I mean."

Jenny followed Megan's gaze up the line, where Europa Griggs could be seen, fresh from driving duty, rubbing her backside as she limped along.

Jenny laughed. "Guess so!"

Up ahead, Jason had more pressing matters on his hands.

Salmon Kendall's wagon had run over a rock—a big one—and broken an axle. Jason had the Kendalls unpacking their wagon, and Jedediah had hastened the other wagons in the train around the Kendalls, in order to keep the time lost to a minimum. Jason was helping Kendall to lighten the load while he waited for the Griggs's wagon or the Wheelers to arrive.

At least, Seth Wheeler had said he'd done some blacksmithing and wheelwrighting in the past, and Milton Griggs was a smithy. Jason hoped that included some axle work, too.

When the Morellis passed them, Doc hollered, "Can I help, Jason?" but Jason waved them past. That was all they needed—a wagon falling on their only medical man. He noticed that the MacDonalds passed them by without a word. That figured. Even the Milchers called, "God be with you!" And the Nordstroms offered their help, but not so much as a look from Hamish MacDonald. Or Matthew, who actually could have been of some help.

But no, he just rode that big flashy pinto of his right on past, as if Jason and the Kendalls and half their cargo, spread out in the grass, weren't there at all.

Bastard.

When the boys driving the cattle and horses came up close, Ward Wanamaker rode over and pitched in, and together, he and Jason and Salmon got the wagon unloaded at just about the time that Seth Wheeler drove his team up.

When he asked if he could help, Jason sure didn't turn him down.

"Wagon's got a busted axle, Seth," he said, while Wheeler climbed down. "I'm hoping you can do something about it."

Seth gave a scratch to the back of his head. "Lemme take a look," he said, and got to it.

After five minutes of making sounds to himself and peering from various angles, he stood erect. "Can't fix 'er," he said, and Salmon's face fell. "But I can shore her up long enough to make the town. Your papa said there was a town not too far off, right?" he asked Jason.

"Sure did."

"Good. Don't supposed anybody in this train has an anvil? And supplies?"

Jason brightened. "Milton Griggs does, I'm pretty sure. He's comin' up now."

Through the dust came the Griggs wagon, with an uncomfortable Milton driving, his lank blond hair flopping beneath his hat. Jason flagged him down and explained the problem, and he and Milt and Seth wrestled the anvil out of the back of the wagon.

"You're lucky that thing didn't go straight through the bed," Seth remarked.

"Bottom's reinforced iron," Milt replied with a grunt.

"The whole thing?" Jason asked. He wondered that

the horses could haul it. That is, until he took another look at the team. They were Belgian draft horses, as big and muscular as the man who owned them.

"Whole thing," Milt said. "Somebody got a fire goin'? I got my bellows and stuff in here somewhere. . . ."

"Not much to it, Mr. Griggs," said Seth. "We've just gotta strap her together with some iron. They can replace the axle when we get to the town, I hope. This thing's pretty much shot."

"Call me Milt," Griggs replied. "Let's get that fire going. C'mon, boys, somebody dig me a pit."

Salmon Kendall's wagon, jerry-rigged axle and all, fell into last place in the train an hour later. His load had been split out between Milt Griggs and Seth Wheeler—and Saul Cohen's extra rig—and the wagon slowly limped along, eventually catching up with the others.

Jedediah rode back to see how they were doing, and was pleased to see that Jason had handled the situation. "How's that axle look?" he asked as they rode along, bringing up the rear.

Jason thumbed his hat back. "Not good. They'll have to replace it once we get to town. Either that, or buy a whole new rig. If I didn't know different, I'd swear that Conestoga of Kendall's was a hundred years old. Damn thing's full of dry rot."

Jedediah made a disapproving face, then shook his head. "Idiots," he muttered.

Jason knew exactly what he meant, and didn't reply.

They pulled into the tiny prairie farming community of Bliss, Kansas, just as the sun was setting. Jedediah ordered the wagons lined up along the outskirts of the tiny town, and the herd bedded down farther out.

Jason rode in ahead to see if they had a carter or a smithy who could either fix the wagon or replace it. He was hoping for the first, and he knew Salmon Kendall was, too. Wagons cost dear, and Salmon didn't look as if he was any too flush. He'd sweated all through the repair work, and Jason was pretty sure it wasn't from the heat.

He found Bliss Livery right off, and as it turned out, he was in luck. The proprietor had nothing of the sort handy, but he knew of some folks that had come out from Iowa not too long ago, and were trying to sell their wagon. When Jason tracked them down, it turned out they were just as willing to sell the whole shebang as the rear axle. He guessed they weren't doing too well, by the look of them.

He rode the palomino out to meet Salmon Kendall, and directed him out to the wagon, then sent Milton Griggs after him, just in case. They might need another pair of strong shoulders, and frankly, Jason wasn't up to it.

He'd yanked his neck, back, and shoulder clear out of kilter back there, while they were shoring up the axle. So far, he'd managed to hide it from his father and the others—who wanted a ramrod who busted his own body during the first days out?—but right now, all Jason wanted was a hot bath in town, to soak in for maybe six or eight hours.

That, and about a quart of liniment.

Jason wasn't accustomed to hurting himself. Oh, he'd been shot during the War, but that had been an accident of friendly fire, seeing as how he was attached to the Department of War in Washington. Just a glorified paper-pusher, that's all he'd been. Not a hero, like his brother, butchered in the swamps of Georgia, or a hero like his father, who'd spent the last few months of the war in that hellhole, Andersonville Prison.

No, just a pen-pusher, a paper-shuffler, a requisitions expert—a big, fat nothing.

The man who'd shot him was a private, cleaning his mostly-for-show service pistol in the next office over.

Life wasn't fair, Jason thought grimly as he rode into town and found the barbershop. No, sir, it just wasn't fair at all.

Jedediah was just sitting down to his supper, and wondering what the devil had become of his son, when he heard a wagon rolling in, and saw Salmon Kendall on the driver's bench. Salmon reined in the team and jumped down, a grin splitting his face.

"What do you think, Mr. Fury? Isn't she grand?" He swept an arm back toward the big Conestoga, which was quite obviously a different rig than the one he'd been limping along in.

"Why, I think she's a beauty, Salmon," Jedediah replied, and fought off the urge to scratch his head in wonder. Salmon and Cordelia Kendall hadn't a pot to piss in nor a window to toss it out of. How on earth could he have afforded a new rig?

"Mr. Kroeger, the man with the wagon?" Salmon went on, all in a rush. "He and his folks are havin' hard times, said that if he couldn't sell the wagon, they were going to burn it for firewood this winter. Wouldn't sell just the axle. So I traded him, my wagon for his, and I threw in a hog for good measure. What do you think of that?"

Salmon's hogs were fat and would make a lot of bacon and chops, and Jedediah knew the Kendall kids had named them, but he kept his counsel. "That's fine," he said, "right fine. Griggs look her over for you?"

Salmon gave a quick, happy nod. "Yes, indeed, and he pronounced her trail-worthy—a good deal better than my other rig, he said later on. I mean, after we left the Kroeger place. Why, he said my old rig was full of dry rot."

Jedediah nodded. "Happens. You'd best get your things unloaded from the other folks' wagons and into your own before they start to take a dislike to you, though."

"Certainly, certainly!"

As Salmon Kendall climbed back up to the driver's bench, Jedediah called after him, "You haven't seen my boy, have you?"

"Not since about five. He rode off toward town."

Jedediah nodded, as if that was exactly where Jason was supposed to be—blast him, anyway!—and waved to Salmon as he pulled out.

"Papa?" asked Jenny, sitting at his side. She had perpetrated the so-called stew on his plate. He probably could have sold it for axle grease, if it had a little less salt in it.

"What, baby?"

"What's Jason doing in town all this time?"

"I'm sure he's got a good reason, honey." He held out his plate. "Now, serve me up some more of that cornmeal mush."

Jenny sighed. "Corn bread, Papa. Corn bread."

5

Jason was slouched in the steaming tub, half asleep, his back and shoulder having already been tremendously eased, when the voice broke into his consciousness.

"You the wagon man?"

He opened one eye, surprised to hear the female voice in the men's bathing house, but not entirely shocked by it. During the War, even lowly paper-pushers were welcome in Washington's bordellos. And it was precisely the tone of voice he'd expect to hear in one of those places, too.

The woman standing at the doorway was dressed like a saloon girl. Probably was one, too, in those bright green spangles. And all that red hair, piled up on her head. She couldn't be much older than he was, even under all that makeup. Which she didn't really need, he caught himself thinking.

He opened the other eye.

"Yes, I guess I am," he said. "Miss . . . ?"

"Miss Krimp," she said. "Abigail Krimp. And you are?"

"Jason Fury, Miss." He caught her gaze flicking to the tub, trying to peek beneath the water, and set his sponge drifting to cover a strategic part of his anatomy.

She looked disappointed.

He smiled. "And may I ask what brings you . . . here, Miss Abigail Krimp?"

"My man would'a come, but he was busy. Sort of. So he sent me."

She was pretty enough, but if she didn't come to the point pretty soon, he was liable to toss that wet sponge at her. "About what?"

"About joinin' up!" she said, as if he should have read her mind.

"With the wagon train?" he asked. She sure didn't look like any pioneer he'd ever seen.

"Well, of course." Rather than showing signs of leaving, she sat down on the bench and crossed her arms stubbornly. She cocked her head. "You're a handsome devil, ain't you? And we wanna go to California, me and Rome. Be nice, havin' you along for scenery the whole way."

"And Rome is?"

"My man, you fool. The one playin' cards up at the Red Garter."

Now, Jason didn't have anything against gamblers, personally, but he knew his father did. Jedediah vowed, quite often, as a matter of fact, that they were all larcenous ne'er-do-wells and he wouldn't have one within five miles of any of his wagons.

So Jason pursed his lips for a second, then said, "I'm afraid you'll have to find yourself a different party to join, Miss Krimp."

This time, she shot to her feet. "Why?"

"Because my pa is in charge, not me, and he doesn't take to gamblers of any sort. Or fancified ladies," he added.

Suddenly, she looked stricken. "But there hasn't been a wagon train through here in two years! They all go down through Hastings!"

"Then I suggest you get yourselves down to Hastings, wherever that is."

She yanked a folded towel off the shelf behind her and threw it at him. "Well, I guess that 'handsome is as handsome does' is the truth, after all!" she spit. "Thank you very much, and good luck with your journey!" she added snidely before she flounced out of the bathhouse, emerald skirts flashing.

He caught the towel before it could land in his bathwater, and set it on the little tub-side stool that also held an empty shot glass and a half bottle of bourbon.

"Thanks, Miss Abigail," he said to the place where she'd been, then closed his eyes and sank back down. "I'll probably be needing it. Sooner or later."

Women. Were they all crazy, or was it only the ones he ran into?

Roman LeFebvre sat back and watched the rube in the blue shirt scrape up the pot. Rome was having a bad night, and he should have bowed out of the game a good hour ago. Really, he should have gotten out years ago, but if a man was born stubborn, he couldn't help but hold onto it.

He was going to have to let go, though. All he had left was the hundred-dollar bill pinned inside his vest, and he'd need that to pay the hotel bill and get the rig out of hock, down at the livery.

He was saved from having to ante up again by Abigail's entrance into the saloon. He stood immediately when she stepped in, bowed out of the game, and made his way over to her through the crowd.

But when he got to her, she didn't have good news for him. He knew it by the look on her face, which he promptly backhanded.

Holding a hand to her cheek, she flushed red and looked around, embarrassed, then said, "It wasn't my fault, Rome. He said they didn't take gamblers."

He slapped her again, although no one in the bar paid any mind to it. This time, she fell back against the bar and began to cry. "I'm sorry, Rome," she sniveled. "It wasn't my fault, I tell you."

He raised his hand again, but this time withheld it when she cowered. "Get packed," he said. "Everything. Swipe the hotel linens, too." He started toward the door.

"Wh-where you goin'?" she whined.

He should have traded her off to that whoremonger down in Louisiana when he had the chance, he thought. But he hadn't, and now he was stuck with her.

"To do some business," he said. It was none of her nevermind, anyway. She ought to be happy he was going to take her along with him.

Midnight at the sleepy line of wagons, and Salmon Kendall was still too excited to sleep. Carefully, he slipped from under the drowsing Cordelia's arms and crept from the wagon, careful not to wake the children.

The night air was cool and crisp, so cool that he almost needed a jacket. He would have gone back up for it, too, except he saw a fire still burning down the line. Someone else couldn't sleep, either. He headed for it. Perhaps they'd have a spare cup of coffee.

To his surprise, he found Saul Cohen crouched near the fire, intently gazing into a small book. Cohen looked up. "Evening, Mr. Kendall," he said.

"Evening, Mr. Cohen," Salmon replied, then gestured with his hand. "May I?"

"Sit, sit!" said Cohen, and closed his book. He tucked it in his pocket. "And what keeps you from sleep this night?"

Salmon smiled a little. "My new wagon. Still can't believe it."

Cohen shrugged. "Why not? All the way since Maryland, we've seen them rotting in the fields. Once a man has got to where he is going, he does not have much use for a Conestoga. Unless, of course, he's in the freight business . . ." He stared into the fire, as if he were considering just that.

For a moment, Salmon felt a little cheated. And stupid, because now he did remember seeing all those wagons left out in the fields, in various stages of disrepair and decay. But then Cohen said, "So, you'd like coffee?"

"Yes, please, Mr. Cohen. If you wouldn't mind." Salmon like the way Cohen talked. It was kind of singsongy, sort of like German but with more of a thickness to it. Or something. He couldn't quite peg it.

"My name is Saul," Cohen said.

"And I'm Salmon."

The two men shook hands before Cohen handed over the mug, which Salmon took happily. He said, "Well, I s'pose I ain't the best businessman. I'm just happy I got the problem solved. Mr. Griggs said my old wagon would have just . . . *disintegrated* before we got to Colorado!"

Cohen nodded. "Dry rot?"

"How did you know?"

Cohen shrugged. "It's a gift."

Salmon laughed nervously, then sipped at his coffee, more to keep his mouth busy than because of overwhelming thirst. He didn't know quite how to respond.

Saul Cohen, who didn't seem aware of his discomfort, said, "You are a brave one, coming to drink coffee with me, even in the middle of the night. Don't you think that Milcher will be cursing your milk cow tomorrow?"

Salmon blinked in surprise. "We only have the one, and he's a bull."

"Still, he would try to curse him. Or maybe your chickens . . ."

"Why?"

It was Cohen's turn to blink. "Salmon, my friend, don't you know that I am a Jew?"

"You are?"

Cohen said nothing.

"But we used to live down the road from some Cohans, and their people came from Ireland!"

"Cohen, Cohan, so much difference one little vowel makes. . . ."

Salmon shook his head. "Well, I'll be dogged. I'll be double dogged!" He had never before known a Jew, but Saul Cohen didn't look like he ate babies or anything. If a body listened to Milcher, well . . . Then he mumbled, "Aw, that Milcher's an idiot. 'Tween you and me, I don't even think he's a real man of God."

"I am inclined to agree," Saul said, adding, "Sometimes, on these old Conestogas, the linchpins give out. You have a problem like that, you come see Saul Cohen. I'm no good for axles, but linchpins, I can replace. And for you, wholesale." He waved an arm toward his spare wagon, the one Salmon knew was loaded down with hardware.

"Thank you, Saul. I'll keep that in mind."

The two men smiled, having come to an unspoken agreement of friendship. It was the first, on the trip, for Salmon. He'd bet it was for Saul, too.

Salmon leaned back and took another swig of coffee, but this time it had nothing to do with nervousness. "That chicken your wife fried up for my family tonight? It was right good. Like for you to thank her for me. Those potato things were real tasty, too."

Saul nodded. "It was for her own happiness. She knew all your family's cooking things were spread out in other wagons. Besides," he added with a tip of his head, "you go to all the trouble to kill one chicken kosher, you might as well kill two."

Salmon chuckled, although that *kosher* part had him stumped.

"And of course," Saul continued, "they were your hens. We should be thanking you."

Salmon's chuckle turned into a roar that was broken only by his wife's hissed, "Salmon Kendall! What are you doing out here in the middle of the night?"

He looked up and there she stood, cloaked in her old wrapper, her night-braid looped over her shoulder, glowering at him.

He scrambled to his feet. "Sorry, Cordelia," he whispered. And then he remembered himself. "Saul, this is my wife, Cordelia. Cordie, Saul Cohen."

Cordelia nodded. "A pleasure, Mr. Cohen. I've met your wife, Rachael. She's a wonderful cook."

"Saul," Cohen said. "And yes, my Rachael knows her way around a hen." He, too, got to his feet.

Cordelia smiled and said, "As you were, Mr. Cohen. I just came to rope my husband and bring him back to pasture."

Cohen slid back to the ground gratefully. He lifted a hand and said, "Good grazing, friend Salmon." Then the hand went to his pocket, and he pulled out that slim volume again.

"You, too, Saul," Salmon replied as he walked away, backward, with Cordelia resolutely pulling him along. "See you tomorrow!"

They were nearly to the wagon before Cordelia hissed, "You're making friends with him?"

Salmon put on his brakes, which nearly hauled Cordelia off her feet. He was a good foot taller than she.

"Why not?" he asked.

"Well, they're Jews, Salmon!"

"So?"

"Reverend Milcher says they killed our Lord!"

"I don't know about that, honey. And I'm pretty dang sure Saul Cohen didn't do it personally. Why, his wife made us dinner!"

"But the Reverend Milcher says—"

"You know, I'm pretty sick of the Reverend Milcher and his sayings. He's not even a good Baptist! He's not anything that I can figure. And he's tryin' to run everybody in this group."

"He's a good Christian man, Salmon."

Salmon sighed. "Not if he's holdin' it against the Cohens that a bunch of Romans crucified Jesus nigh on two thousand years ago. That's just plain stupid. Besides, I like Saul."

"But—"

"Stop bein' silly, gal." He patted her fanny. "Now, get yourself up in the wagon before you wake the whole camp."

6

Two days out of Bliss, Kansas, Jedediah waved Jason to his side. He'd had a gnawing feeling that somebody was following them, but he'd only just seen the trace of a dust cloud on their back trail. Whoever it was, there weren't very many of them. However, he didn't like anybody riding his coattails, be it for good or for ill, and he intended to find out what was going on.

Jason rode his palomino up alongside Jedediah's roan. "What is it?"

No *Papa*, no nothing. No respect!

But he didn't take the time to jaw out the boy. He pointed to the low ridge they'd just traversed. "See that dust cloud?"

Jason squinted and shaded his eyes with the flat of his hand, scouting along the horizon. Finally, he stuck out a hand, pointing. "There?"

"Right. Somebody's dogging us. Take a man off the herd and ride back. See what it is they want."

"And if they want to rob us and take our livestock?"

"Guess you'll have to stop them, won't you?" Jedediah wheeled his horse and took off at a slow lope, toward the head of the train.

Jason sat there a moment, shaking his head. Everything was so cut and dried, so black and white, with his father. What was he supposed to do, just ride back and shoot whoever it was? That would make Papa proud, now wouldn't it?

Sniffing disdainfully, he at last turned his horse toward the herd, which was traveling off the wagon train's right flank. He loped on out to its edge, to Ward Wanamaker, who was riding a sorrel today. Ward reined the gelding in as Jason joined him.

"My father thinks we've got company coming up behind," Jason said without preamble. "Ride back with me and take a look, okay?"

"Sure," Ward said amiably. "But I can tell you right now what it is."

Jason cocked a brow.

"Buggy," Ward replied to the unspoken query. "Fella and a gal, and the back's packed full of their stuff, includin' three crates of chickens and a goose, and about six pink trunks."

"Pink?"

"Pink."

"Redheaded woman?"

"Yup." Now it was Ward's turn to arch his sandy brows. "You know who it is, Jason?"

"Think so," Jason said, disgust dripping from his voice. His pa wasn't going to be happy about this. He reined his palomino around and said, "C'mon."

The two men rode down the line of wagons at a soft lope, until they left the caravan behind and headed out over the open, empty prairie, toward the distant ridge and its thin skyward trail of dust.

Jedediah rode up next to the Kendall wagon, spotted Salmon on the driver's bench, and called, "How's the new rig working out for you?"

Salmon's face lit up just like a kid with a new toy.

"Just fine, Mr. Fury, just dandy! She's sure a lot smoother, though I suppose these help some." He pointed down to the folded blankets, quilts, and coats upon which he sat.

Jedediah said, "You're catching on, Kendall."

He let Kendall pass him while he looked back down the line. He saw Jason and Ward in the distance, heading back toward whoever was trailing them.

He figured it was somebody looking for a little free protection.

Probably not Indians, who wouldn't trail them for so long or so openly. The same went for raiders. Anyone counting on doing harm to the group would have done it long before now, and they sure wouldn't have been so dumb as to give themselves away by sending up a careless cloud of dust.

No, Jason and Ward would be all right.

He dug his heels into his roan and urged it up the line again, past Salmon Kendall, past Saul Cohen's two wagons, past the MacDonald rig, and up to the Milchers. Mrs. Milcher and all the kids were on foot, and the reverend was driving one-handed, smoking his pipe.

"Afternoon, Milcher," he called, tipping his hat.

"Good day to you, Brother Fury," came the answer.

Briefly, Jedediah ground his teeth. He'd just about reached the end of his rope with Milcher's affectations. He said, as evenly as possible, "Why don't you let your two littlest gals ride? They can't weigh much." Their mother was practically dragging them through the prairie grass.

"No, it's good for them, brother," Milcher replied. "Children need their exercise, just as young animals do. Makes them strong in their bodies, and strong with the Lord! Have you thought any more about Sunday?"

"I told you before, Milcher, this train doesn't stop for a whole day for anything, not even God."

"But the spiritual needs of—"

"You can meet those in your own time. Mine is going to be spent moving this train west."

He didn't bother to say good-bye. He simply let his roan drop back to poor, beleaguered Lavinia Milcher and reached down. "Hand 'em up, ma'am," he said, nodding to the girls, and one at a time, she lifted them up to him.

"Thank you, Mr. Fury," she said. "They're exhausted."

"It's a long walk for a little mite," he said as he got the girls adjusted behind the saddle. "Hang on tight, now!"

He dropped back further, to the MacDonalds' wagon. He wasn't fond of Hamish or his son, Matthew, both of whom were on horseback, at the head of the train. They were already hard at work establishing themselves as "community leaders," Jedediah thought with a snort.

But Megan was driving their rig right now, and she was as unlike her father and brother as a strawberry was from two sour pippins. Jedediah didn't think she'd mind the two little ones.

He was right. She accepted them with open arms, and let them crawl back inside the wagon, where they could lay down. They were asleep almost before their heads were down on the pillows.

"That reverend!" she whispered, so the girls couldn't hear. "He's just too pious to breathe!"

"I wouldn't argue that, Miss Megan," Jedediah said, gave one last glance toward Jason and Ward's diminishing figures, then rode off to fill in for Ward with the herd.

"I told you, lady, you're not welcome. Not you *or* your gambler friend."

The girl—Abigail Something-or-Other, he remembered—stared up at Jason dumbly. The slicker at her side was looking pretty annoyed, though. They didn't even come close to having a proper rig.

"But here we are," said the man, finally. He gripped his buggy whip like a cudgel. He was fairly tall, dark, and good-looking in a way that would have done him quite a bit of good on a riverboat. But not out here.

"That doesn't have anything to do with it," Jason insisted. "Turn around and go back while you still can."

"No," the man said, and he said it like he meant it.

Ward wasn't being any help either. He just sat there on his sorrel without saying a peep, and his attitude seemed fairly sympathetic toward the pair in the buggy.

Jason leaned forward in his saddle, elbows out, palms crossed on the saddle horn. He could sit here arguing with them all day, but he could see this fellow was so set on westering that they'd still follow along. He supposed he could just shoot the man, but then that would leave him with the gal on his hands and probably no way to get her back to a town. So he did the next best thing.

"All right," he said. "I'll let you talk to the wagon master." He wheeled his horse and set off at a gallop toward the train, which was out of sight. Ward came right along with him, and he heard the rattle and bang of an overstressed buggy trying to keep up behind them.

He allowed himself a little smile. The jolting ride up to the train ought to knock some of the pioneer spirit out of them. He glanced back just long enough to glimpse the woman holding onto the armrest and seat back for dear life, and the man braced stiffly—only his feet, pushing against the footrest, and his mid-back, pressed as if his life depended on it against the backrest, were still—both of their faces filled with sheer terror at being jolted skyward at any moment.

Smugly, Jason urged his mount into a faster gallop.

Within a few minutes, they were even with the train and had come up even with Jedediah, who had dismounted and was staring very unkindly at the newcomers.

"Get them the hell out of here," he said.

It seemed to Jason as if his father had taken all of fifteen seconds to evaluate the pair of interlopers. It was longer than he'd expected, actually.

"Told 'em, Pa," Jason said with a shrug, "but they wouldn't take no for an answer."

"That's right, Mr. Fury," Ward added. As if Jason needed backing up.

Still, he was glad for the words. His father looked uncommonly angry, which was very angry indeed.

"We don't want your . . ." His father trailed off, interrupting his famous "We-Don't-Need-Your-Kind-Around-Here" speech, and Jason noticed that his gaze had been momentarily distracted by a passing wagon. Milcher's wagon. And Milcher was staring down at the girl and her spangled dress like the very wrath of Judgment itself.

Jedediah seemed to gather himself. He looked the man in the face and asked, "What's your name, boy?"

"Roman LeFebvre," came the reply, "and my lovely companion is Miss Abigail Krimp. And I am hardly a boy, sir, although I thank you for the compliment."

"None intended. Everybody under forty is a kid to me." Jedediah idly scratched at the back of his neck, which Jason knew meant his pa was brewing up something.

"Tell you what, Roman LeFebvre," Jedediah finally said. "You fall in behind the last wagon. Once we camp for the night, we'll let the group decide whether you stay or go. Their decision's final, no ifs, ands, or buts. Fair by you?"

"Delightful, and fair as a Kansas court. And call me Rome, sir."

Jedediah stepped back up on his roan. To the complaint of saddle leather, he said, "Last wagon, Rome."

His father rode off in one direction, Ward rode off to join the herd, and LeFebvre turned his wagon around to meet up with the end of the line, which left Jason sitting there on his horse, watching the line of Conestogas move on by while he slowly shook his head.

7

The Reverend Milcher took center stage after dinner, just as Jedediah had thought he would. As for himself, Jedediah leaned back against the wheel of his wagon and lit his pipe, getting ready for what would pass as his evening's entertainment.

"Now, you all know me, my dear friends," the reverend began, sweeping his arm toward the crowd in a semblance of humility. "I have brought most of you from the eastern shores of our great country. I have ministered to your needs and seen to your wants."

A few heads nodded in agreement, but nobody said anything.

"And I say unto you that these newcomers have no business amongst us. We are stalwart and godly men and women, pioneers all! We have no need for spangles and cards, for games of chance and ribald song."

Fewer heads nodded this time and a few folks frowned, but he wasn't getting any argument from anyone yet, Jedediah noted. He wondered if Milcher thought that the gambler was going to turn his wagon into a traveling honky-tonk, while his women played "Belly Up to the Bar" on Milcher's wife's damned piano.

"And I say, so long as we are cleansing our ranks, we should divest ourselves of the members of the Hebrew race amid our ranks. Let these crucifiers of Christ and these ... entertainers ... be cast out together, so that they may have each other's company on the return trip. I am not an unkind man, my friends. I would send no one into the wilderness alone."

There was a profound silence, during which you could hear only the stomp of a horse's hoof and the soft grunting of a pig.

And then Salmon Kendall, shy and quiet Salmon, stood up.

"Brother Kendall!" announced Milcher, obviously expecting a second to his motion.

"Excuse me, Reverend, but I don't know what you got against the Cohens here. Why, Saul and his Rachael have been good friends to me and mine!"

Thus began a heated debate that delineated—for Jedediah, at least—the two major camps among his pilgrims. Namely, those who wished to cross the land lugging a cross and the New Testament, and those who just wanted to get there, period.

Now, the MacDonalds—two of them, anyhow—were staunchly on Milcher's side. Surprisingly, so were the Wheelers, the Widow Jameson and her brood, and Milt Billings, although as a hired man, Milt had little say-so in the actual proceedings.

Dr. Morelli and his family kept their mouths firmly closed—afraid, Jedediah supposed, that if the Jews and the "fancy women" and gamblers were being picked on now, the Roman Catholics couldn't be far behind.

He probably wasn't wrong.

When you came right down to it, Jedediah was rooting for the gambler and his woman. Oh, he didn't like them. He didn't have to, he supposed. But it'd be worth the extra bother of taking the gambler along if it knocked the Reverend Milcher down a notch.

Jedediah would like that. In fact, he'd enjoy it more than he'd admit, even to himself.

They went on and on, these hearty pioneers of his,

these escapees from civilized society. They argued and yelled and preached and hollered as if they were debating the course of the world instead of just one lonely wagon train of outsiders, of dreamers. And that was it, wasn't it? No matter what each one thought, no matter from whence he or she had come, they were all outsiders now. Outsiders, wherever they went.

And at long last, the outsiders voted to keep the Cohens, to keep the gambler and his woman, and to ignore Reverend Milcher's protests to the contrary.

Jedediah had good reason to smile.

He stood up, brushing his hand on his britches. "Glad that's settled," he said. He knocked his pipe's bowl against the palm of his hand. "One more thing before everybody turns in for the night." He threw a glance Milcher's way, to make sure he was paying attention. This was mostly for his benefit.

"I noticed a lot of little kids really dragging today," Jedediah said. "This is probably my fault for not saying something sooner, but I make it a rule on my drives that all kids under the age of ten walk only half days. It's too hard on them, otherwise. Everybody got that?"

The Reverend Milcher sniffed and disappeared into his Conestoga. But he'd heard.

"LeFebvre!" Jedediah shouted, waving a hand at the gambler.

LeFebvre, a winner's grin stretching his face, came at a trot. "Yes, Mr. Fury! What can I do for you?"

"You can pay me your share of my fee," Jedediah said, and stuck out his hand while he looked over the man's poor excuse for a rig. "That'll be eighty dollars, flat."

Abigail hummed to herself as she finished cleaning the supper things. She'd listened to the debates earlier, and was more than pleased that they wouldn't have to turn back, although she was more than a little miffed by Milcher's use of the term "ribald song."

She wasn't exactly sure what that meant, but she figured it couldn't be good, not judging by the tone he'd used.

Rome was still up there, talking to the wagon master, Mr. Fury. She'd learned he was the pretty boy's father, and she sighed without realizing it. That was one fellow she'd like to take a little buggy ride with, if it weren't for Rome.

Oh, well. Things were what they were. Rome couldn't keep her from looking, though.

Suddenly he was behind her, grabbing her around the waist.

"Oh!" she gasped.

He chuckled into her ear. "Oh, indeed, Abby!"

She relaxed a bit. He was in a good mood.

He let go of her just long enough to turn her about to face him. "You got any pin money, sweetheart?" he asked with a smile.

"There's thirty-five cents in my pocketbook," she replied.

His grip on her arm tightened. "No, I mean real money. It's gonna cost us eighty bucks to tag along with this crew. After I paid the hotel and the livery, I've only got forty left. And that's just barely."

Her arm was already throbbing, and her eyes welled with tears. "Rome, really, I—"

"You must have something stashed, honey. Something put by. How'd you buy that new dress? The green one? I sure didn't shell out for it." He began to slowly twist the gripping hand, and now her arm burned as well as throbbed. She thought she might faint.

"In my carpetbag," she whispered, afraid that at any minute she'd scream and give them away.

"That's my girl," he said, dropping her arm like she were nothing more than a rag doll. If she hadn't had the corner of the buggy to catch herself on, she would have fallen like one.

"Why do you have to be so mean to me?" she asked, rubbing her arm.

He already had her carpetbag, and was dumping its contents out into the dirt. "Because you don't tell me the truth, angel," he said, distracted by the bag. He pawed through her underwear and shoes and stockings until he found her little change purse, the one made out of soft deerskin with silver fittings.

He opened it and smiled as he counted out the money.

"You been holdin' out on me, Abby," he said at last. "Seventy bucks, even." He stuffed the whole roll in his pocket, then stood up. "I'm gonna go pay Fury. You clean this mess up, you hear?"

As he strode off, out across the circle made by the wagons, she heaved a sigh, then bent to pluck her clothing from the dirt. And as she did, her tears finally spilled. He'd taken her money, her savings. She'd never be free of him now. At least, not before three or four years more of working in saloons and brothels.

She'd been barely sixteen, orphaned, and living on the street when he found her and introduced her to the life, and she knew nothing else. It was a rough and cruel existence, and she had secret dreams of leaving it behind, of marrying, of becoming respectable. Now she'd be too old for anyone to want her. At least, by the time she saved up enough money to slip out of Rome's clutches.

Blast him, anyway.

She stuffed the last items into her bag, realizing that tomorrow she'd have to figure out how to do laundry on the move. She looked out, into the open circle, and saw young Jason Fury talking to another man, the one with whom he'd ridden out to their buggy. Ward Something? It didn't matter. The two of them were standing before a fire, and the light washed up over Jason, all golden and warm and enticing.

It wasn't difficult to imagine him making love to her, being tender and gentle and caring and . . . nice. Yes, nice.

He was looking better and better.

"Well," Ward was saying as they watched the gambler walk past them, "I guess they're stayin'. Your old man sure surprised me!"

"You're not the only one," Jason said. The only thing he could figure out was that his father was, in some way, using Rome and Abigail to put the Reverend Milcher in his place. If so, it had worked as far as he could tell. Milcher sure had his drawers in a bunch.

Which was just as fine with Jason, if the truth be told. He couldn't abide the man.

But then, he didn't like much of anybody on the train. There was an open, ongoing aggravation between him and Matt MacDonald. It was only a matter of time before it would come to blows, and everybody knew it.

He found Mr. Nordstrom haughty and stuck up, the Mortons—every single one of them, including Milton Griggs—too boring for words, and Eulaylee Jameson (and all three of her grown kids) too bigoted and narrow-minded to live.

And the rest of them, he didn't know well enough to dislike. He figured he would in time, though.

But he thought he kind of liked Ward Wanamaker, and he knew he liked the oldest Milcher boy, Tommy— probably because he was a frequent target of Matt

MacDonald—and he was certain that he liked Megan MacDonald. The girl was pretty, with long, shiny, setter-red braids, sparkling green eyes fringed with russet lashes, and a fair, freckled face. And she made him laugh.

She was only seventeen, though, and so he hadn't made any overtures. Only seventeen, and bound to stay with her family out West, once they got there. He'd be headed back East. To college. Which was no place for a married man.

"What?" he said. Ward had been saying something or other, and Jason had completely lost track of it.

"Indians?" Ward said. "Where were you? Rhode Island? I asked if we should we count on a fight anytime soon."

Jason shook his head. "Hard to tell. Before the War, we could buy most of 'em off with cattle or trade goods. That's been years ago, though."

Ward nodded. "So you know 'bout as much about it as I do."

"I'd say you nailed it, Ward."

Saul and Rachael Cohen lay snug in their quilts, having tucked their three boys into the spare wagon and seen them safely asleep. Saul was pleased about the evening's goings-on, although he was sorry the subject had come up. Again.

"Will it ever stop, Saul?" Rachael asked, echoing his thoughts.

"You expect it to stop?" he replied. "How can it stop while these *goyim* are still so ignorant? Since the beginning of time, they've been ignorant. You think anything will change that?"

"I suppose you are right," she said, and snuggled closer to his side. "But still, I will pray for them."

He smiled. "Now you're sounding like Reverend

Milcher, Rachael, always praying for people. Who don't want to be prayed for, I might add."

"Possibly, Saul," she said, cocking a brow. "But *I* have a more direct route." Before he could speak, she closed her eyes, and whispered, "No middleman."

8

Three weeks, one broken leg, a busted collarbone, and one Piute episode later, the wagons found themselves cutting down into Indian Territory.

Electa Morton had tripped in a gopher hole and broken her leg below the knee, and was now teaching school from the back of her parents' wagon. Young Tommy Milcher, Jason's friend and admirer, fell from his horse and broke his collarbone.

As for the Piute, they had been a small band of stragglers, and had been bought off with the offer of three of Jedediah's "eating steers" from the herd, two blankets, and one hand mirror from Jedediah's box of trinkets. They'd ridden off, happy as larks.

But Jason was concerned. The wagons would be going through Comanche territory, and nobody but him seemed the least bit upset about this. Even his father, usually a most careful guardian, seemed unconcerned. Maybe Jedediah knew something he didn't.

He sincerely hoped that was the case.

They were two days into Indian Territory, and their surroundings had gradually changed from the endless grasslands of Kansas, where they had gathered buffalo chips for fuel to burn and bumped across seas of buffalo bones, to a rugged kind of half-desert, half-plains. The kids were more often riding than walking, even more than his father had decreed the night he had the blowup with Milcher.

Well, not a blowup, really, Jason corrected himself. It had been more like a quiet victory, without a threat made or a single blow struck.

But Milcher had been halfway quiet ever since, with the exception of Sunday mornings. Roman and Abigail had been left alone, and the Cohens had been unmolested, insofar as he knew, by either hand or word.

Hamish MacDonald, however, was becoming more and more of a problem. He had his own map, and it was his dogged persistence that had them taking this particular route. Jedediah had wanted to stay either further north or cut down further south—mostly to avoid the Comanche threat—but Hamish swore up and down that he had it on good authority—from his brother-in-law, who had settled in Houston some years ago—that lately, the whole Indian problem was much exaggerated, and mostly a fabrication of the Eastern newspapers.

Jason was surprised his father hadn't fought harder against Hamish. But he hadn't, and for the first time, Jason wondered if perhaps his father was getting too old for these trips.

Jason was out riding with the herd, and they were slowly moving over a hill of red earth about two hundred yards north of the wagons. Grazing had been good for the livestock so far, and they were all fat and sleek. He knew that wouldn't last long, though. The grazing was growing sparse, and would continue to grow thinner and thinner.

He swung farther to the north to bring in a stray calf when he caught a movement from the corner of his eye.

It wasn't much. Just a patch of color that shouldn't have been there. And he could no longer see it.

But he'd been well trained by his father, and he immediately called to Ward. "Get the herd down the hill!" And then he bolted down himself, toward the train, chasing the errant calf before him.

He came down so fast that his mare nearly skidded into the side of the MacDonalds' wagon, and he immediately shouted, "Circle the wagons in tight! Men, get your firearms ready!"

He cantered down the line shouting the same thing, over and over, to the shocked faces of the pilgrims, but they all sped up and made a halfway decent circle up ahead. He heard his father shouting instructions, too, while the herd of horses and cattle and such climbed down the hill and headed for the circle. The men left a gap between two wagons just wide enough to funnel the herd through, three and four at a time, then closed it tight as Jason galloped back.

It was just in time, too. He heard the whoops of attacking Indians breasting the hill's crest just as he jumped his palomino over the traces of Rome LeFebvre's silly little buggy. Leaping from the saddle and slapping his palomino on the backside, he crouched down beside Rome. His pistol was in one hand and his rifle was in the other.

All Rome had in his shaking hands was an old Colt Navy and a derringer. Abigail was crouched beside him, white with terror.

Jason saw their attackers now, and too clearly. They came boiling down the hillside in full battle regalia, with very serious looks on their painted faces.

Jason had met up with Comanche once before. He hadn't liked it.

He pulled up his rifle and drew a bead on one of the front riders. He fired.

And missed.

He cranked another shot into the chamber and aimed again.

This time, his slug hit home.

By now, the suddenly formed camp was in a panic. Some of the men were doing as Jedediah had instructed back in Missouri—firing while their wives or kids reloaded. Others, including Roman, were simply frozen.

Jason wasn't one to waste time. He slugged Rome in the jaw, just hard enough to get his attention, and said, "Shoot, you idiot!"

When that didn't work, he shouted, "You know what a Comanche'll do to you if they get in here? They'll tie you to a wagon wheel, cut a hole in your belly, string your guts out while you watch, and let the pigs eat them while you're still living!"

Rome went to work with his gun. Abigail fainted.

Jason just kept on firing.

He fired, in fact, until he ran himself out of ammunition and had to make a run across the circle to the ordnance wagon. On his way, he dodged confused cattle and spooked horses, jumped over a dog, snatched up a wandering Milcher kid, and took a stray arrow just above his left elbow.

He handed over the Milchers' spawn, then reached across his body and broke the arrow off, so that only an inch of it protruded from his flesh. It was bleeding like a butchered hog, but he didn't have time for it now.

His father, who had obviously run dry himself, was at the ordnance wagon, and tossed him down a box of the right ammo for his rifle. His eye flicked to Jason's arm and he opened his mouth, but Jason shouted, "It's all right, Pa! Watch yourself!"

And then he headed back across, to the sounds of Indian whoops and cries, shouted curses, kids and women crying, and cattle and horses dying. He ducked down behind Salmon Kendall's rig. Salmon needed some help.

His wife, Cordelia, lay behind him, struck by a

Comanche lance. Dead. His daughter, Peony, lay across her mother, sobbing. Salmon and his boy, Sammy Jr., both had rifles and were firing with a grim purpose. Sammy Jr.'s face was streaked with tears, but his expression was resolute.

Salmon just looked like he was in shock. Load, fire. Load, fire. Load, fire.

But he was accurate. Before him lay four dead Comanche, one of whom had made it halfway past the wagon's whiffle bar. It was likely the Indian's lance that had killed Cordelia, Jason thought.

Quickly, he knelt beside Salmon, shouldered his rifle, and took a shot at the swiftly circling Indians. "Should have got yourself a repeater!" he shouted.

"No money!" Salmon shouted back as he reloaded. And fired again. He was a good shot, all right. Another Comanche dropped from his pony.

"Sorry about your wife," Jason added lamely.

Salmon paused, mid-reload. "Yeah. Those red sons of bitches!"

All business once more, Jason shouted, "Your kid isn't hitting anything. Have him load for you instead."

"Sammy!" Salmon barked, and it was done.

Across the circle, Jedediah had located Milt Billings, the only man of them who spoke any of the Comanches' lingo. Milt was emptying his handgun into the swarm at the time, so Jedediah waited until he stopped to reload.

"Milt!" he roared, to be heard above the noise of the battle. "Milt! Can you talk to these Indians? Tell them we'll give them cattle!"

But Milt, concentrating on loading his gun, simply shook his head. He looked up and shouted, "No way these boys are gonna settle for anything but the whole herd, goats, pigs, and all. And the girls."

Jedediah's blood ran momentarily cold. He'd known what the Comanche were after, but hadn't wanted to admit it to himself, hadn't wanted to believe their luck could be that bad. Why had he let Milcher and MacDonald talk him into taking this bloody route, anyway? If they got out of this, he was going to ride into Houston, Texas, himself, and take a good, hard kick at Hamish MacDonald's brother-in-law's backside.

Maybe his head.

And then he felt a sharp pain in his side.

"What?" he asked, much more softly than he'd intended.

He tumbled backward, and was lucky that his fall was broken by a steer who didn't step on him, once he was down. Suddenly, he couldn't see very well, which was strange because he'd always had eyes like an eagle.

Maybe it was later in the day than he'd thought.

Maybe it was getting dark.

That was good, wasn't it? The Comanche would break off their attack, come nightfall.

Vaguely, distantly, he heard someone shout, "Mr. Fury! Somebody get Dr. Morelli! Dear God, Fury's down!"

And then he heard no more.

Jason was over by Carrie English's wagon, helping Carrie and her daughter put some sort of system in place, when Morelli came for him. He had just about decided to send Gil Collins, one of the hired men, down to help her. She was a widow, and she was a lousy shot.

Someone put a hand on his shoulder, and he wheeled, nearly shooting Morelli in the chest. Morelli quickly blocked the rifle's barrel with his forearm—his quickened reflexes arising from the heat of the battle—and said, "Come with me, Jason."

When he added, "Now," Jason took him seriously, and shouted his apologies to the Widow English, adding that he'd send her some help.

Morelli said no more, just shoved his way through the milling, excited herd, leading a puzzled Jason. If there was something wrong, why hadn't his father taken care of it? He stopped following Morelli's relentless path when he spotted Gil Collins, who was helping the MacDonalds, who probably needed the least help of anybody. Both Hamish and Matthew were firing, taking down their share of the redskins, with Megan reloading like a maniac.

He shouted until he got Gil's attention, then told him to go help out down at the English wagon. And then he stood there, being shoved around by crazed cattle and spooked horses, until Gil got on his way, taking Megan along with him. Gil was a cipher, and Jason suspected he was a bit of a slacker, too, something they could hardly afford right now. But Megan was a fine shot, when she was allowed to do something besides reload.

Quickly, he caught sight of Morelli, who had paused and was waving at him frantically to hurry along. The roar of battle assaulted his ears as he pushed forward again, leaping over dead and dying livestock, shoving the living ones out of his way. He fervently hoped they weren't losing as many people.

And still, the whoops and screams and battle cries came. He suddenly realized he had no idea how long the battle had been raging.

Forever, maybe.

When he caught up with Morelli, he was standing over a prone, blanketed figure, and the bottom dropped out of Jason's stomach. The toe of his father's boot protruded from one end.

He said, "It's not . . ."

Morelli had the grace to look uncomfortable as well as saddened. "I'm afraid so, son. Your father took a lance through the lungs. There was nothing I could do."

Jason barely had time to absorb this—that his father, who had joked that he'd been through things that would have killed most men twice, yet lived to tell the story, could actually die—when a great roar and cry arose from the east side of the circled wagons.

Jason saw that the circle had been breeched beside the gambler's rig, and that there were Comanche inside their camp, driving out livestock, and taking captives. Women screamed in terror, girls cried hysterically as they were snatched up into the arms of mounted heathen, as men and boys alike tried their best to hold back the seemingly endless horde.

A tomahawk swung, and young Tommy Milcher, the boy that Jason had saved from a beating by Matt MacDonald, back in Kansas City, fell dead, his head nearly separated from his body. A lance split the air, and fatally pinned Miranda Nordstrom to the side of a wagon. Her husband, Randall, screamed and ran to her, putting a slug squarely through the neck of the brave that had killed her.

By the time Jason, Dr. Morelli, Hamish MacDonald, and Saul Cohen hastily worked their way through the terrified livestock, the Comanche were already riding off and had cut off their attack. They had a small herd of horses and cattle—"Got three of my goddamn Morgans!" Hamish shouted—and a small number of the older girls that had been at that end of the circle.

"I'd think you'd be more concerned about your daughter, Hamish," Jason said, clipped and hard, and began searching for Jenny. His sister had been wearing a yellow dress, he remembered. Where in that milling mob of confused and heartbroken settlers could he glimpse even a flash of that color?

Hamish set in to search, too, shouting, "Megan! Megan, girl, answer your father!"

Jason could find that yellow color nowhere in the camp. But as the Indians breasted a distant hill, he saw it. She was slung across an Indian pony, and as far as he could tell, she was still fighting her captor.

Good girl.

Good Jenny. She was a Fury, after all. And it was up to him to save her.

9

Jason barely gave Morelli time to get the arrow out and patch up his arm before he was in the saddle. The weeping of women was all around him, and the silent tears of the men he felt, more than heard.

Lord knows, it was all he could do to keep his own tears back. He had lost his father and his sister, all that remained of his entire family. But he wasn't alone, he kept reminding himself. Nearly everyone had lost someone—man, woman, or child—either to the lance or the arrow or the blade, or to the kidnapping.

Milt Billings, the man who spoke Comanche, came along, as did Ward Wanamaker. They had to go along, because they worked for the Furys, which meant they now worked for Jason. And, oddly enough, Saul Cohen tagged along. Jason couldn't figure what Cohen was trying to prove, but he wasn't about to turn down any volunteer.

Except Matt MacDonald. Jason didn't want to ride with anybody who'd screw it up, which was something Matt was bound to do.

Instead, he told Matt and Hamish that he needed them both at the wagons. They were both good shots, and the Comanche could well come back.

And they bought it.

But Jason knew there wasn't a chance in hell

those Indians would return. They'd gotten what they wanted.

He gave orders that the dead be buried, the injured be taken to Dr. Morelli's wagon, which was serving as their hospital, and that the dying livestock be put down as painlessly as possible.

He also gave orders that somebody get the dead steers dressed out and start them to roasting. He didn't want anything to be wasted. They'd need that meat.

Through the twilight, Jason and his group rode over the same hills the Comanches had traveled with their prisoners. Through the night, under the moon and the stars, they followed the savages' trail.

And then finally, at about three o'clock in the morning, they were just breasting a rise when Jason whispered, "Down! Everybody get down!"

He had spotted the camp.

Ward took the horses back down the rise and out of sight, while the other three men lay on their bellies, scouting the camp with binoculars or spyglasses.

Down below, all was quiet. Only a couple of small fires were still burning themselves out. There were a few teepees set up, but it didn't look to Jason like any sort of permanent camp. Probably just a raiding party.

"There's our stock," whispered Saul, at Jason's right. He pointed quickly to the northeast.

Sure enough, their cattle and horses, along with the Comanche ponies, stood quietly, dozing within a crude corral their captors had tied together from the plentiful tumbleweeds. It was staked, at intervals, by lances thrust down through the thickest part of the sage.

As Ward Wanamaker joined them, Milt Billings said, "This is gonna be easy."

Jason, lowering his spyglass, twisted toward him. "Easy? Just how is that?"

Milt looked at him like he was an idiot. "We just sneak down and drive off all the livestock."

"And what about the girls?" Saul asked.

"Oh," Milt said, and looked away. "I forgot about them."

Jason turned back to the camp and raised his glass again. "You've got too much of your mind on MacDonald's Morgans, Milt. You'd best be thinking about his daughter, instead."

Saul Cohen asked, "So, is anyone hatching anything close to a plan? I'm thinking that maybe we should just ask them nice, but then again, I'm thinking that's probably the best way to get them mad again."

"Don't take much," said Milt.

"Nope," echoed Ward, who was obviously at a loss, too. "Maybe Milt didn't have such a bad idea, Jason. I mean, Mr. Fury." This last part he added quickly, as if he'd just remembered Jedediah was dead, and now Jason was the top boss.

"It's still *Jason*." he said. "And you mean we should use that as a diversion?"

Ward nodded.

"Been thinking the same thing, myself."

"It could work," Saul said, sounding very unconvinced. He shrugged. "Or not."

"Guess I ain't so stupid after all," Milt muttered beneath his breath as the four of them backed down the slope.

Twenty minutes later found them creeping along the outside fringes of the camp. So far, so good, other than the camp cur that had started barking. Milt's cranky, growled "Shut up, dog!" in Comanche had quieted him, though.

Jason was in the lead, and he had just reached the makeshift corral. He pulled the knife from his boot and cut the first thin strip of buffalo hide that held the brush together, when he heard a scuffle behind him.

He wheeled to see Ward Wanamaker down on the ground, fighting off a Comanche warrior. He ran back toward Ward, knife in his hand, when he was bushwacked by yet another brave and went sailing to the side. He hit the ground rolling, and brought the point of his knife up just in time. The young brave who had bowled him over stopped his attack quite suddenly, and stood there, a rifle in his hand and just out of reach, smiling.

Jason didn't think that smile of his was any too wholesome. Neither was the rifle, come to think of it.

He heard a yelp behind him as Saul Cohen was taken down—not permanently, he prayed. He could see Ward and Milt. Ward was on the ground. Milt was kneeling, head down. A Comanche blade was at his throat, and he looked like he was waiting to die.

He was likely the only sensible one among them.

Jason's pa had always said he didn't have much sense, though, and he wasn't ready to give up. To the young Comanche standing guard over him, he said, "Speak any English? You savvy American?"

The brave remained silent.

"Milt!" he called.

Haltingly, a knife pressed to his throat, Milt repeated his question in the Comanche tongue.

Jason's guard barked something back to Milt, who answered him carefully. Then Jason's guard lowered the muzzle of his rifle, just a touch.

"You are Fury?" the brave asked, and Jason realized that as big as the brave was, he wasn't just young, he was a kid! And then he realized the boy had spoken in English.

"Jason Fury," he said, trying not to let all the surprise he felt show in his voice.

"A relation to the Fury called Jedediah?"

"My father," Jason replied, and couldn't keep the bitterness from his voice.

The brave didn't seem to notice, though. "I am son of Peta Nocona, Chief of the Quahada Comanche. My father knows your father, and is friend to him." The rifle's business end dropped a tad lower.

All of a sudden, Jason's future didn't seem so dark. He said, "Then you must be the one called Quanah Parker. My father spoke of you and your father. He traded with you often." In fact, Jedediah Fury had been one of the only white men who could ride in and out of Peta Nocona's camps, and keep both his hair and his intestines intact.

Quanah stared at him for what seemed like hours— but was probably mere minutes—then waved his rifle. "Why did he not come?"

"He's dead. Your raiding party killed him."

A few minutes longer of staring. No remorse, no apology, just that blank stare. Then Quanah said, "Stand up, Jason Fury. You are in no danger. Yet."

Once Jason got to his feet, he saw that although tall and imposing in physique, the boy was about sixteen or seventeen years old—and had light eyes. His father had mentioned those disconcerting eyes more than once. They were a steely gray, a legacy from his white mother— Cynthia Ann Parker, Jason thought it was. She'd been a captive, too, just like their girls.

Jason started to sheathe his blade back in his boot, but Quanah shook his head. "Drop it to the ground. Your guns, too." He barked a command at one of the other Comanches, and they all motioned their captives up, too, and divested them of their weapons.

They were making enough noise that the camp was waking. A few braves appeared at the flaps of their teepees, ready for action, but Quanah made sure they knew everything was under control.

"Why have you come here tonight, Jason Fury?" he asked. "Why have you come to steal our horses and cattle? You come to revenge your father, maybe?"

"I came to retrieve what was stolen from me," Jason said. He knew that if he gave in, even an inch, he'd be seen as weak.

"I've come for my cattle and my horses and my sister. My father's life cannot be taken back."

Quanah's brows shot up, and his smile widened. He swept an arm toward the slowly milling animals in the corral. "All these are yours? Will you play for them, Jason Fury?"

"Play what?" If this Indian thought he was going to sit down at a spinet and play "My Old Kentucky Home," he was out of his mind.

Quanah started walking, and motioned Jason along. They were of a height. "I have learned a new game," Quanah said, "from our friends in Mexico."

Jason's mind was suddenly flooded with what might define a game for Quanah, and his blood nearly froze in his veins. His father had told him plenty of stories about the Comanches' penchant for cruelty as sport, even cruelty to their own dogs and horses. He shuddered, but he followed Quanah inside a tent anyway.

Quanah motioned for him to sit down on the buffalo-hide rug that made up the floor, and it was only once he sat that he noticed Saul, Milt, and Ward come into the tent behind him. They squatted down next to him, in a line to his right.

Poor Ward looked like Jason felt—terrified. Milt looked

resigned, as if he'd already given in to destiny and just wanted to get it over with. Saul, on the other hand, seemed fascinated with everything he saw, from the feathered headdress hanging back against one curve of the teepee's side and the scalp locks depending from Quanah's spears, to the tent itself. He seemed to be making mental notes on its construction.

The warriors who had been guarding them followed them inside, making for a cramped tent, and sat down behind them, still holding their own guns on them.

Not the most auspicious setting for a parlor game, Jason thought.

While Quanah threw some sticks on the little fire that had been dying in the center of the tent on a broad stone hearth of sorts, he said something in Comanche, and all of a sudden Milt smiled a little. The braves behind them lowered the weapons they held, and seemed to relax. One even stifled a chuckle.

Well, Jason thought, at least it wasn't going to be a blood sport. The man behind him would have allowed himself a big belly laugh for that.

Quanah turned to Jason. "You play the game called craps? Blanket dice? Do you know it?" He gestured with his hand, as if he were throwing dice.

A few years in Washington, D.C., had taught Jason a lot of things his father wouldn't have approved of. He nodded. "I've played once or twice."

"Good," Quanah said. "I find it most amusing." He spoke quickly in his tongue to the other Comanche, all of whom hurried from the teepee.

Milt leaned toward Jason and said, "I'll be a badger's butt. He's sent 'em to wake the others, in case anybody wants to make side bets."

"You have dice?" a smiling Quanah asked, as if he were under the impression that all white people carried them by the bushel basket.

Most whites of Quanah's acquaintance probably did, Jason realized. The Comancheros, whites who were known to trade with and raid along with the Comanche, were a pretty rough bunch.

"You could be holding your horses for a minute?" said Saul's voice.

10

Jason looked down the line. Ward shrugged. Milt shook his head. Saul rooted in his pockets.

"Saul?" said Jason.

"No. I have no dice," he answered. "But maybe I have something almost as good." And with that, he produced three sugar cubes from his pocket. "These will do, no?"

"Aw, there ain't no dots on 'em!" Milt sneered.

"There can be," Saul said, inspecting the cubes and discarding the one with the most wear on the edges. He held the remaining two out to Ward. "You'll hold, please? Lightly, so they shouldn't melt?"

Ward reluctantly took the cubes, and Saul went back to patting his pockets—this time, the ones on his vest. He finally came up with a few toothpicks, and smiled. He took the sugar back from Ward, and proceeded to go to work, drilling shallow, precise holes in the cubes with the end of a toothpick, then gathering a tiny bit of ash from the edge of the fire, and inserting some in each hole. Not much. Just enough to darken it.

When he was finished with the first, Jason held out his hand. "Can I see it?" he asked, and then turned it over in his hand, inspecting it closely. "Saul, this is a work of art."

Saul, working intently on the second cube, simply shrugged and said, "My Uncle Amos, he was a jeweler," as if that explained everything.

By that time, there was quite a crowd gathered outside the tent's flap. Jason heard muted voices muttering in Comanche, and an occasional chuckle. His gut tightened. He'd already lost his father this night. Now, he was gambling his sister and Megan MacDonald on the roll of a couple of sugar cubes.

Someone had brought the girls, too. They were shoved into the tent behind Jason and his three companions. Jenny, true to the Fury family temperament, looked mad as hell, but that didn't stop her from giving him a quick hug and whispering, "I knew you'd come. Where's Papa?"

He said, "Later, Jenny," and chanced a glance at Megan. She looked confused and a little teary, but not beaten. *Good girl,* he thought. The third captive was Deborah Jameson, youngest daughter of the widowed Eulaylee Jameson, and Deborah was the next thing to hysterical.

"These three are my first wager," said Quanah Parker, now deadly serious. "What do you have to match it?"

"All our firearms," said Jason.

"You forget, Jason Fury. We have already taken your firearms."

Jason acknowledged that with a brief nod. He didn't have a single thing on him worth trading. He looked at the men. Even Saul, who he was beginning to count on to get him out of rough patches, held his hands to the side, palms up. Nothing.

And then he had something akin to a stroke of genius. "We rode here on four horses, and one of them is a palomino mare. Only four years old, top stock. Will they do?"

Quanah nodded. "Is good enough. I would like to see this mare."

Jason shook his head. "Not unless you win them."

Quanah laughed, surprising Jason. "You are smart, like your father," he said at last. "You roll first."

Saul handed Jason the sugar cubes, saying, "They're not ivory, you know. Don't toss them too hard."

Jason nodded.

He took the homemade dice and shook them gently in his cupped hands. Then he closed his eyes, said a short prayer, and tossed them down in front of him.

He heard a shout go up outside before he was able to pry his eyelids open. Quanah sat, shaking his head slowly, while Saul and the others grinned from ear to ear, and Jenny suddenly hugged him from behind. One die read six, the other five. He'd won.

Thank God.

He whispered, "Jenny, is there anyone else?"

"No, just us three," replied his demolisher of kitchens and ruiner of meals. "Jason, you're wonderful, even if you're my brother!"

"And now I shoot," Quanah said, collecting the sugar cubes. He looked frustrated, and a little angry. It was not a handsome expression on one so young. "This time, it is the . . . stolen horses against your women."

"Cattle *and* horses," Jason said, "against our horses. *Just* our horses."

"No." Quanah's cold, gray eyes narrowed. "The women, too."

Nothing was more important to Jason than getting those girls safely back to camp. Not even Hamish MacDonald's fancy Morgan mares. "I guess we're done, then," he said, and started to get to his feet.

But the point of a spear against his shoulder sat him back down again. He didn't know who was holding it, but it didn't matter.

"This time, I roll," Quanah said, and Jason prayed fervently for a two, three, or twelve. You lost automatically if you rolled one of those.

The dice stopped rolling on the buffalo hide. A four and a two: six.

Quanah Parker shouted something in Comanche, and there was a lot of noise outside. Milt leaned toward Jason and muttered, "He said, the point is six. Or somethin' like that."

Quanah waited for the noise, presumably of side bets being made and covered, to die down, then gently shook the sugar cubes again. Jason heard Saul mumbling, "Seven, seven, seven, seven . . ." as though praying. Seven would be the only automatic loser Quanah could roll.

But Quanah heard it too. "Quiet!" he roared, and the spear point that had been pressing against Jason's shoulder suddenly arced overhead and landed next to Saul's throat. He gulped audibly and his eyes grew round, but he shut up.

Quanah threw the dice again.

Ten.

The warrior with the spear called the news outside, and again there was a noisy roil of voices.

Finally, Quanah called for silence, and rolled the dice again.

Eight.

This went on for some time, with Quanah trying to roll his "point" of another six, and failing each time, between bursts of activity outside the tent flap, while Jason and his men all silently prayed he'd roll a seven.

After rolling his third ten, Quanah threw the dice down and leapt to his feet. "These are loaded! You try to cheat me!"

Jason, to whom he'd made the accusation, forgot about the brave with the spear, and jumped to his feet, too. Once he was standing, though, he felt its tip press hard into his back. But one shouted, angry word from Quanah, and it pulled away. From the corner of his eye, Jason saw the spear-holder back out of the tent.

"Back with the women!" he said, and the men rose

and began to back up. "All except you!" He pointed to Jason.

"You think I loaded sugar cubes?" Jason asked. "How the heck could I do that? They weren't mine, and playing craps was your cockamamy idea in the first place!"

From across the tent's tiny fire, Quanah launched himself at Jason. He landed with the force of a charging bull, and Jason was knocked to the ground, narrowly missing Megan, who scrambled aside and sent Milt sprawling into Saul.

Quanah's hands were round Jason's throat, throttling him, and Jason did the only thing he could think of: He brought up one knee, hard, between Quanah's legs. The pressure of Quanah's fingers immediately left Jason's throat as Quanah doubled up with pain.

Still gasping for breath, Jason took advantage of the situation and pulled Quanah back down by his beaded neck-piece, rolling atop him at the same time. Then he hauled off and punched him in the face, just as hard as he could.

"Jason, don't!" he heard Jenny cry out, but he hit Quanah again.

Quanah wasn't out, though, and when Jason came in to deliver the third punch, Quanah blocked it with a massive forearm, which then drove upward to clip Jason under the chin. It hurt like hell.

The blow knocked Jason upward and halfway out of the teepee, and when he looked up, he found himself surrounded by at least twenty angry braves.

From inside, he heard Quanah bark a command, and the crowd stepped back. Jason barely had time to make a sigh of relief before the gray-eyed brave was on him again. The two rolled about in the dust of the camp, slugging, slapping, kicking, and generally trying their best to murder each other, when Jason caught a glimpse of the opening of Quanah's teepee.

What he saw only made him madder.

Here he was, getting beaten to a bloody pulp and creating the world's greatest distraction, and there stood his entire party, girls included, watching the fight and cheering him on, when they could have been sneaking off to the horses.

He slammed Quanah with a hard right to the ear, and Quanah rolled him farther, catching him in the temple at the same time. One of the braves threw a knife down to Quanah, who snatched it up and held it at Jason's throat. Jason felt it break the skin, felt rivulets of blood flow down the sides of his neck.

He did the only thing he could think of. He smiled and said, "Your point was a six, Quanah?"

Suddenly, the blade eased away and Quanah barked out a laugh. He sat up, still holding the knife—which was, at least, now pointed to the side—then slowly stood up. "You are right, Jason Fury. It was a six."

He tossed the blade to the side, then held a hand down to Jason, who gratefully took it. When both men were on their feet, they dusted themselves off and checked their body parts for serious injury, and Quanah was still laughing. Jason couldn't help himself from joining in, although in his case, it was the sheer ridiculousness of the thing. Why Quanah was laughing was anybody's guess.

Maybe he was thinking of all the good, clean fun his boys would have later on, torturing them.

But instead of throwing Jason on the fire, he escorted him back to the teepee they'd tumbled out of, and resumed his former position. Jason and his people did the same.

"Jason, are you hurt?" Jenny asked.

"Are you all right?" Megan echoed.

Deborah Jameson didn't speak to him. She was too busy weeping.

"I'm fine," he replied, even though his throat stung like the devil and it felt like his jaw was broken.

After a few moments, Quanah found the dice again and inspected them for serious damage. Fortunately, they were the only things in the teepee that had escaped it.

With a grunt, he threw them again.

An eight.

He frowned, then gathered them again. Jason noticed that all this tossing and the friction with hands and the buffalo hide had worn the sharp edges of the sugar cubes away. There weren't many more rolls left in them.

Quanah muttered something, then threw the dice.

Jason held his breath.

"Seven!" shouted Saul, then clamped a hand over his own mouth.

"Seven it is," muttered Jason, who couldn't believe his luck. Now, of course, he had to be even luckier to get everybody, along with the livestock, out of the village and home safely.

It wasn't difficult at all, though. Quanah was a man of his word. They gathered the horses and cattle, including Saul's bullock, which his kids had named Mr. Cow—and which Saul greeted with a happy hug—and MacDonald's Morgans, and Jason left three of their meat steers behind. In the end, they had about fifteen horses and cattle to drive back to camp.

They rode out of the Comanche enclave fully armed and with no problem, gathered up the horses they'd ridden in on, and started back to the camp. It was coming dawn by then, and Jason was discovering new bumps and bruises every minute.

The girls were asleep on their horses by the time they came in sight of the circled wagons, but the drifting scent of roasting beef brought Megan around first.

"Food?" she asked, her pretty face soft and fresh with sleep.

"Likely more of it than you'll ever want to see again," Jason replied. He saw kids and women turning four steers on long spits over roasting fires in the center of camp, and men hitching a team to a dead horse, presumably to drag the corpse out of the camp, where they'd already dragged three others.

Dr. Morelli was still hard at work. He looked to be setting one of the Milcher kids' legs. Jason also saw Reverend Milcher out south of the wagons, presiding over the burials of the butchered whites.

Milcher was good for something, anyway.

11

In the privacy of their wagon, Jason held Jenny tightly against his chest. She wept as if her heart was broken, which it most probably was.

"Hush," Jason soothed. "Shh, shh, baby girl."

"But why!" she cried. "Why didn't you tell me?"

"Because I thought it was best, honey," he whispered. He had been exhausted last night, and they'd never have made it back to the wagons if he'd told her about Pa. He was exhausted now, but didn't have any further to go. He just had to comfort her the best way he knew how.

"Jenny, you've got to be brave," he said, although he didn't alter his embrace. "We've all got to be."

"Why?" she beseeched him. "Papa's dead, Jason! Papa's dead. . . ."

She fell into another fit of weeping, and still Jason held her, trying by his actions to let her know that she still had somebody, even if it was only her lousy older brother.

Megan MacDonald, red-eyed and looking overly hugged and squeezed after her reunion with her father and brother, poked her head over the tailgate's edge.

"Excuse me, Jason," she said softly, "but you should come."

He still cradled his sister's head. "What is it, Megan?"

She climbed up into the wagon and made her way to

him and Jenny. "Go see Dr. Morelli," she said, taking a sobbing Jenny into her own arms. "Now."

Once she'd given Jason time to get well clear of the Conestoga, Megan held Jenny away, at arm's length. "Jenny, listen to me," she began. When Jenny, lost in sorrow, paid her no mind, Megan shook her roughly, then slapped her across the face.

This finally got her attention.

"Ow!" Jenny exclaimed, holding a hand to her damp cheek. "Why did you do that? How can you be so mean to me?"

"Jenny, you're not the only one," Megan said, her voice soft. "We all lost someone, be it friends or family. And Jason, who was in here comforting you? Well, he lost his daddy when you did. Did you stop to think of that? Did you stop to think that he might miss him even more than you do? That the weight of being in charge and the responsibility of all of us is on his shoulders, now?"

Jenny slowly blinked.

"I don't mean to scold, Jenny," Megan went on gently. "I just think you should look at things from, well, a broader perspective, that's all."

"I-if I'd stayed in Kansas City, like Papa wanted, I wouldn't know about this. I wouldn't have had to know until Jason came home."

Jenny's voice was getting a little too floaty and far away, just like Mrs. Halliday, back home, right before she went crazy and took an ax handle to the family cat.

Megan said, "Don't you go getting ax-handle crazy on me, Jenny."

Jenny squinted at her curiously.

"I need you to get your grieving over with. *Jason* needs you to be done with it, or at least put it aside for a while, and come help up clean up after those blasted Comanche. The horses and cattle kicked everything to pieces last night. And the Comanches will be riding in here in a couple of hours to pick up their dead. Jason's going to need all the help he can get."

"But I'm so tired," Jenny croaked.

"Me, too."

Slowly, Jenny nodded.

"I'm going to leave you alone now, all right?"

Jenny whispered, "Yes. Thank you, Meg."

"You're welcome, honey," Megan said, and brushed a kiss over Jenny's forehead before she climbed over the seat and back down to earth. She heard Jenny's renewed weeping from inside the wagon, but at least it was more controlled, less wild, than it had been before.

It was true that Megan had lost friends in the raid, but no family, thank the Lord. But then, it was also true that Mr. Fury had been like a kind and good father to them all.

She looked across the circle to see Jason, Dr. Morelli, and the Reverend Milcher engaged in discussion, and set out at a brisk clip to join them. Or at least get within eavesdropping distance.

This ought to be a scrap worth hearing.

"You know, Milcher," Jason said in a conversational tone, "I've been trying to be nice to you on account of your losing Tommy, who I had a high regard for, myself, and your two younger boys getting hurt. But I'm just about ready to haul off and slug you."

Milcher had the audacity to look both surprised and offended. "Whatever for, sir?"

"You know damn well what for. You are not going to pile up those dead Comanches like so much kindling and set fire to them!"

"They're heathen," Milcher said firmly. "Murdering, thieving heathen at that. It's all they deserve."

Jason paused for a moment, his jaw muscles working overtime.

"Now, Reverend," interjected Dr. Morelli, "Jason said that the other Comanche were coming to pick up their bodies. We can't have them find a pile of ashes, now can we? Why, there's likely to be another massacre!"

"We're all shook out of shape, Milcher," Jason said, under control again. "We don't want to do anything that we'll be sorry for later. Quanah showed himself to be a fair man, last night, and I—"

"A fair man?" Milcher shouted. "Since when are any godless redskins fair men? Since when do those who murder and steal qualify as men at all? They killed my son. Do you hear me? My *son*! The one who did it could be right out there!" He swept his arm around the circled wagons, to where the corpses of the Comanche lay.

"When you find the one who did it, do you want to carve him up a little?" Jason asked. "Maybe take his scalp? Maybe hack off his balls?"

Milcher suddenly looked horrified.

Morelli muttered, "Now, Jason . . ."

"Go back to your wagon, Milcher," Jason said, "and think about turning the other cheek. Either grab some of that beef that's roasting, or comfort your wife—she lost Tommy, too, you know—or get some shut-eye. But when those Comanche show up to gather their dead, I do *not* want to see your face."

When Milcher climbed back up into his wagon, he immediately embraced his grief-stricken wife.

He looked about him as his children, who were mostly whole—other than the nine-year-old boy with a broken arm and the seven-year-old boy with a bandaged calf where a heathen arrow had found home and the fifteen-year-old boy who would never be with them again, never see the distant shores of California, never again join him in prayer—and the Reverend Milcher collapsed into tears, muttering, "Oh God, my God . . ." into his wife's shoulder.

Alone, his hat in his hand and the noonday sun beating on the back of his neck, Jason slowly walked down the line of fresh graves. Someone had made crosses and simply written the names of the deceased. No niceties like dates of birth or death, no "beloved son" or "devoted wife." Just last name, first initial.

Here lay, now and forever, T. Milcher—plucky young Tommy; M. Nordstrom—quiet, plain-faced Miranda, who sewed like an angel; C. Kendall—Cordelia, wife of Salmon and mother to Sammy and Peony; R. LeFebvre—Rome, the down-on-his-luck gambler; S. Wheeler—Seth, part-time blacksmith and wheelwright, who had dreamt of opening his own saloon; M. Griggs, who had died from his wounds while Jason was playing dice with Quanah Parker; and, at the end of the row, his father.

J. Fury, the marker said. Except, in Jedediah's case, someone had taken the time and care to carefully write "Wagon Master & Good Shepherd" underneath in tiny, precise letters.

Obviously, someone who also had not thought highly of Hamish MacDonald's all-knowing brother in Houston. Or maybe it was his brother-in-law. At this point, Jason didn't much care.

All he knew for certain was that what he was left with was at least as many injured as killed, wagons with nobody to drive them—although he figured to leave Abigail Krimp's buggy behind and have her drive the

Nordstroms' second wagon, the one that the late Miranda Nordstrom had been driving.

A picture flashed through his head, that of poor, plain Miranda, pinned to the side of a wagon by a Comanche spear, the life draining from her face.

He shook his head like a retriever fresh from a pond, as if he could shake that picture, all the bad pictures, from his head. He couldn't, though. He knew he'd live with them for the rest of his life.

"I suppose I should thank you, Fury, for gettin' my sister back safe," said a voice to Jason's left. It belonged to Matt MacDonald. When Jason looked over, there was a smug smirk on Matt's face.

"Consider it said," Jason said, gruffly. A conversation with Matt MacDonald was the last thing he needed right now.

But he quickly learned he was wrong when Matt said, "Pa sent me to get you. We're havin' a meeting. About who should take over now that your pa's dead."

A rush of anger surged through Jason's veins, momentarily replacing his sorrow. He slapped his hat on his head, pushed past Matt, and headed back toward the circle of wagons. "Take over, my Aunt Fanny!" he mumbled.

That big bag of wind, Hamish MacDonald, was behind this. He was certain of it.

12

Jason was right.

When he hopped over the whiffletree of Salmon Kendall's wagon to enter the clearing inside the circle, there was Hamish, standing on a box—which he most likely carried around with him, just to orate from—sweeping his arms back and forth.

Quite a crowd had gathered around him, too.

As he angrily strode out to the center of the circle, Jason flicked his eyes from wagon to wagon, looking for Megan. Surely *she* couldn't be in on this!

He spotted her—sitting beneath Nordstrom's second wagon, knees hugged to her chest and her head bowed. In embarrassment, it seemed. It couldn't be easy having a father like Hamish. It could also be simple exhaustion.

". . . led us into the veritable mouth of disaster," Hamish was saying. He hadn't seen Jason yet. "Don't we need someone trustworthy? Don't we need someone seasoned? Don't we need—"

"Somebody who knows the way?" Jason broke in, from the edge of the crowd.

Chuckles and titters erupted across the throng.

"And somebody who don't have a know-it-all brother-in-law down Texas way," shouted Zachary Morton, their eldest member and head of the Morton clan. His brother's son-in-law had been injured in the fight, and at this moment lay in his wagon, suffering from a stab wound to the chest.

Morton's wife, Suzannah, slapped his arm, but she broke out in a grin anyway. At least, she covered her mouth with her hand, to keep from showing her picket-fence teeth. But her eyes sparkled like a leprechaun's.

"Jason Fury, you're only a boy!" Hamish shouted, and pointed a work-gnarled finger at him.

"Boy, maybe. A fool, no." Jason's temper was about to boil over, and he heard his father's voice in his head, saying, *Calm down, boy, just take a deep breath. . . .*

And so Jason shut up, letting his last comments hang there, in the air. The whole camp had gone quiet, waiting for Hamish's rebuff.

But before he had the chance to formulate something cutting, Jason said, "Everybody, I'd like your attention, if you please. In case you haven't heard, I gave the Comanches leave to come pick up their dead this afternoon, and I reckon it won't be long before they're here. Men, I want you to keep your firearms close at hand, but I don't want anybody flashing them at the Comanches. I want this to go quick and peaceable."

The Comanche arrived within the hour, and so silently that no one was aware of their presence until Milt Billings trotted over to Jason, who was helping Abigail Krimp move her few belongings to Randall Nordstrom's extra wagon.

"They're here," was all Milt said, and Jason looked up to see about fourteen or fifteen braves outside the circle, lifting the bodies of their fallen comrades onto the backs of the extra ponies they'd brought along. Several of the Indian ponies were still aimlessly wandering the scene from last night, and the braves rounded them up, too, and put them into service.

Quanah Parker was with them, which Jason hadn't expected. This was a job you sent your minions to take care of, not one on which you went yourself.

But he was there just the same, mounted on a tall, Medicine Hat pinto, overseeing the others. He caught Jason's eye, and lifted a hand in greeting.

Jason reluctantly waved back. He could tell his men were getting antsy. Even a few of the women looked like they were ready, willing, and able to take on one of those braves with nothing but a couple of darning needles and a frying pan.

When he saw Matt MacDonald slowly pick up his rifle and, from the cover of a wagon, draw a bead on Quanah, he stole up behind him and banged him over the head with the butt of his pistol. Matt crumpled to the ground like a bag of brass doorknobs.

Which got Hamish all bent out of shape. He came charging over, shouting and blustering. Jason turned his gun on Hamish and hissed, "Shut up, you."

Fortunately, Hamish was shocked enough to do it.

The Indians slowly began to make their exit, leading their dead and wounded behind them, but Quanah rode closer to the circled wagons. Right up to Jason, in fact.

"Greetings, Jason Fury," he said, his face like a stone.

"Greetings, Quanah Parker," Jason replied. And waited.

"My braves say your doctor treated the few who still lived after the battle."

He did? thought a surprised Jason. But he didn't let it show on his face. He said. "Our Dr. Morelli is a good man."

"You will give him my thanks, Jason Fury. Until we meet again." Quanah reined his horse in a quick circle and galloped off to join his men.

"Which I hope is the twelfth of Never," Jason muttered.

"When?" demanded Hamish. Jason had all but forgotten him.

"When what?"

"When did that low sawbones sneak out to help those filthy redskins?" Hamish hollered.

Jason realized he was still holding his gun on MacDonald. He said, "Hamish, I haven't slept since yesterday morning. I'm tired and I'm cranky, and if you don't shut the hell up and stop causing trouble, I'm going to pull this trigger and damn the consequences. Do we understand each other?"

Hamish, a glower on his face, remained silent. Which, lucky for him, Jason took for an affirmative. He holstered his gun. "Now, if you want to do something useful, you'll put a party of men together and gather enough kerosene and brush to pile over those dead horses."

"Brush?"

"Yeah. Then set fire to 'em. No sense in drawing in any more predators than we have to. We're not leaving until tomorrow morning."

Dr. Morelli was leaning against a wagon wheel, dozing, when Jason walked up.

"Morelli?"

He cracked open an eye. "Ah, Jason! How goes it?"

"Not too good. Can you take another look at my arm before I go to my wagon and catch some sleep?"

Worry furrowed Morelli's brow. "It's worse? What in the world did you do to it, anyway?"

He asked Jason to remove his shirt, took a look at the wound, and frowned. "Been scrambling around in the dirt?"

"Exactly that," replied Jason wearily. "Plus a few other things."

"Why in heaven's name were—?"

"Don't ask," Jason cut in.

Since Jason looked no more eager to tell him than he did to swim the English Channel, a silent Morelli went to work. At last, after he'd removed the bandages and cleaned the wound with water as best he could, he picked up a bottle of alcohol.

"This is going to sting like hell," he warned, then watched Jason nearly ram his first through his own forehead when he splashed some on the open wound.

"I hear you helped the wounded Comanche," Jason said through clenched teeth.

"Yes," Morelli said, unsure of just how Jason had reacted to that news. "I took an oath to help all those who need my services."

"That was real kind of you, Morelli," Jason said, "and also real stupid. You've got Hamish MacDonald against you now. And more than likely, whoever else he's told."

"I know. I've already had words with Mr. MacDonald." Morelli wouldn't repeat those words for all the money in the world.

Jason seemed to understand. "Erase 'em from your mind, Morelli. I'm in charge, and I say thank you. You did the right thing."

Morelli couldn't help smiling. He tied off the new bandage and quickly fitted Jason with a sling. "Not necessary. Now, get some sleep, son. And throw out that bloody, filthy shirt."

Saul Cohen, who'd slept through the entire day, woke quite pleasantly at ten that evening to find Rachael waving a plate of beef, peas, and potato pancakes under his nose.

"Ah, my beauty!" he said with a yawn.

Rachael smiled. "You're meaning me or the food?"

"I can't mean both?" he replied, and kissed her before he took the plate from her hands.

The boys, all three of them, were curled like dozing puppies at his feet, Rachael was with him, no one was hurt, Mr. Cow was tied to the wagon's tailgate, and the camp was quiet. The past day and a half seemed like some horrible nightmare.

He hoped he'd never have it again.

He and Rachael repaired to the driver's bench while he ate his meal, and afterward, they stayed for a while and just stared up at the moon, drinking some of the sweet wine she'd brought along. They held hands.

"Was it horrible, Saul?" she asked him softly. "Getting the girls and the horses and cattle back, I mean. When you had to go into the Comanche camp."

"Yes and no," he said.

"Why so?"

"Yes, because, my darling, I was so frightened that I almost soiled myself."

She giggled softly. "I think I can understand. And why no?"

He reached into his pocket and produced two much-used sugar cubes.

"Sugar?" She waved a hand at him. "Throw those things away, Saul. They are full of dirt specks from your pocket!"

He held them closer to her. "You're noticing anything out of the ordinary about those 'dirt specks'?"

She took one and held it to her eyes as she twisted it in her fingers. "No, I . . ." And then her brow furrowed. "Saul Cohen! You were gambling?"

He leaned back against the puckered, gathered edge of the wagon's canopy, pulled her close to him, and said, "It's a long and very strange story I'm going to tell you, Rachael Cohen, so you might as well be comfortable."

Beneath her father's wagon, Megan MacDonald feigned sleep. A few feet away, on the other side of the man-height wagon wheels, her father, her brother, and the Reverend Milcher were having a discussion that she was most interested in hearing.

Normally, she wasn't one to eavesdrop, but here she was, doing it twice in the same day. But they'd woken her, and how could she be expected to go back to sleep, especially considering the topic they'd woken her with?

"Well, something's got to be done," the Reverend Milcher was saying. "The boy has no respect for his betters. Absolutely none!"

This had been going on for at least the half hour Megan had been awake.

"I'll agree with you there, Milcher," her father said. She could tell he'd lit a cigar by the meter of his pauses, and also because of the stench the wind wafted her way every once in a while.

"He's an ass," muttered Matt.

"Shut up, Matt," her father snapped. "You got any bright ideas, Milcher? I already tried it the *American* way. Tried holding a meeting and a vote, and what did I get for it? Sass, plain sass, I tell you! It puts me in mind of when I was a lad, in Scotland. Jason Fury's puttin' on a bit of the English, I think!"

Megan knew what he meant by "puttin' on the English"—that Jason was acting like he was better then everybody else—but she didn't agree. Jason *was* better than they were. Out here in the wilderness, at least, and probably anywhere. That wavy, yellow hair and those blue, blue eyes, those dimples and that cleft in his chin and . . .

"You know I would not willingly wish harm on any man, Mr. MacDonald," Milcher said. "It is not the Christian way. And I know that you wouldn't, either."

She heard her brother make a muffled snort, and her father say, "Course not, Reverend. I had nothing so drastic in mind. After all, he saved my darlin' lass, sleepin' there beneath the wagon, from those filthy red-skins. And wipe that smirk off your face, Matthew."

"I'll be bidding you good night, then, MacDonald. I'm afraid that for now, we are in the grips of an ethical dilemma that can't be settled by three men in one night. And I must get some rest. It's been a long day."

"That it has, Milcher."

"May God bless you both, then." The reverend walked away, his footsteps scuffing softly off into the distance.

Megan knew that her father wouldn't do any serious physical harm to Jason. He just wasn't that kind. Oh, he might try to undercut him at any and every given opportunity, and he might even get mad enough to hit him. But he wouldn't kill him. She doubted the Reverend Milcher would even take a swing at him, despite all his complaints. He was too much of a coward.

They just didn't like taking orders from somebody younger than they were, that was it. They were men accustomed to being in charge.

Matt, though, he was different.

Megan loved her brother, but she knew that at heart, he was a bully. And, she thought, he might just be a dangerous bully.

Deadly, even.

Jason had to be warned, and it looked like it was up to her to do it.

13

Jason sat his mare on a ridge not far above the plodding wagons, watching their progress. He was glad they'd left the plains of Kansas far behind. There, one wag had said, you could look farther and see less than anywhere else in the world. Jason had to agree with him.

Kansas, then the Indian Territory, and now New Mexico—beautiful and bleak at the same time.

Since early in the trip and the trouble with Salmon's axle, Jason had been able to avoid stopping near any towns. He did this for two reasons: His father had tended to avoid them, saying that introducing strangers to the mix made for trouble. The second reason was some paperwork that had inexplicably floated across Jason's desk during the War—probably from somebody's attempt to effectively "lose" it.

These papers had told of a wagon train headed west that had cut through the Utah Territory and stopped by a town. A short time after they moved on, they were attacked by what was alternately reported as a band of Indians, or settlers disguised as Indians, or both.

At any rate, the pilgrims were slaughtered, probably by radical Mormons, although the case had never been fully looked into due to the more pressing issues of the War with the South. That had been the Mountain Meadow Massacre.

Jason wasn't taking any chances.

Despite their problems with the Comanche, they were still what would be considered a rich wagon train. They had more than their share of livestock, and between the cloth and so on in Randall Nordstrom's extra wagon and the hardware in Saul Cohen's, the train would be prime booty for any plains pirates that happened along.

There hadn't been any more talk of replacing him since a fortnight past and that Comanche business, although Megan had come to him the next morning. She'd warned him to watch out for her brother, Matt— as if he needed anyone to tell him that—and she'd repeated the conversation she'd overheard between her father, her brother, and Milcher.

He made note of both, however, although he had to admit that he took more notice of how pretty she looked that morning. That, at least, was real and visible. And touchable.

Although he hadn't. One hand had started toward her shoulder, but he'd stopped its movement. There was no future in it, was there? And he was a man intent on realities, on things that were tangible. So he hadn't touched Megan. Not a friendly hand on her shoulder, not a tender, brief brush of her cheek, nothing then, nothing since, because she didn't fit into his plan for the future, the one in which he took these people where they wanted to go, made his way back East, went to college, and then on to big, important things.

But lately, he was having a harder and harder time keeping his hands off her. Hell, he couldn't stop thinking about her. He even dreamt about her, about his lips on hers, about the softness of her throat and the thin, velvet skin of her eyelids. Tantalizing, disturbing dreams of his arms about her, in the night, and what they would do together.

He gave his head a shake, trying to rid it of such

thoughts. He had no business thinking them. What he ought to be thinking about was Jenny.

His little sister hadn't been the same since they'd lost their father. The sparkle was gone from her eyes. He hadn't expected it to return this soon, but he'd thought that he would have seen some hint, some vestige of it at odd, unguarded moments. But no, nothing.

Oh, she went through the motions. She drove their wagon every day, helped make camp at night, helped with the cooking—which, fortunately, had turned into a more communal affair—but she wasn't anywhere near the same boisterous, opinionated, curious, girl-brat Jenny he'd known all of her life.

He was beginning to think that perhaps she'd be better off if he just dropped her off somewhere. He knew a few people along the route, people that he'd trust to keep his only sister safe until he came for her.

Of course, that had been before the War, years ago. There was no telling if any of them were still alive. It was a hard life, west of the Mississippi. And the farther west you went, the tougher it got.

He comforted himself that they'd be out of Comanche territory soon, but then, that only meant they'd be going into Apache country. The Apache weren't that much of a threat, unless, of course, you were a Mexican, a race of people against whom the Apache seemed to hold a special grudge. The wagons would travel south of Tucson through Apache Pass, which was the heart of Chiricahua Apache territory. His father had told him plenty of stories about them, none of them too appetizing.

They were in the New Mexico Territory now. They had just forded Ute Creek with no problem, and were in sight of the Sangre de Cristo mountain range, which at this far distance looked misty and insignificant. He figured to make Santa Fe, just past the southern end of

the Sangre de Cristos, within ten days. That is, if they
kept moving as fast as they had.

This was his one secret pride—that he was making
better time than Jedediah ever had made when ferrying
settlers over the Santa Fe Trail. Of course, outside of
that incident in the panhandle of the Indian Territory.
That had been a piece of really bad luck. Or good luck.

Jason guessed it all depended on how you looked at
it. He'd been tremendously aided by good weather and
a distinct lack of Comanche, which he was beginning to
think might have something to do with Quanah Parker.
They had also been fortunate to find water when it was
needed, when their reserve barrels were nearly dry, and
had been able to find not only enough to drink and
water the livestock, but to refill their barrels completely,
every time.

But he knew that his father would be proud of him.
And for some reason he didn't entirely understand, because he and his father had spent most of their time dis-
agreeing over nearly every conceivable subject, this
gave him a great deal of pleasure.

He'd put Ward temporarily in charge of leading the
train. Milt and Gil could handle the livestock for a while.
The animals were fat, still, and not inclined to be spooky
or stampede. He watched the wagons pass him, swing-
ing south, followed by the herd and remuda.

He sat a moment longer, his thoughts drifting back
to Megan MacDonald, all red hair and freckles and
Celtic charm, and then, finally, he nudged the mare
with his knees, cantering to catch up with the wagons.

The rain started at about three in the afternoon, and
Jason had to choose between trying to hurry the wagons along and thus beat the rising waters to the next

ford, that of another branch of the Canadian River, or stopping exactly where they were in an attempt to let the waters go down again before they reached their banks.

He chose the latter. Wisely, he hoped.

There was no shelter of trees, the terrain being rocky and open, the substrate gravelly, with most vegetation no higher than a bush. Jason circled the wagons as best he could, in the face of what had rapidly become a hard pelt of rain, and brought the herd within the circle. Lightning had a tendency to spook cattle, but when they were firmly surrounded by a comforting fence, or in this case, a circle of wagons, they wouldn't be tempted to bolt.

Rounding up the entire herd tomorrow, if they were hidden in every nook and cranny for three miles around, was the last thing he needed.

He helped a few folks unhitch their draft animals, gave Olympia Morelli a hand with her wagon's canopy, untying it on one side and stretching it out overhead and mooring it by poles to make a covered porch of sorts. It had fallen upon Olympia, along with Rachael Cohen, to do most of the cooking since they were both extraordinary cooks. Oh, the other women helped with stirring or chopping or basting things, but it was those two who kept them fed, preparing the big evening communal meal.

Beneath this canvas-canopied area, Rachael and Olympia set out a large table—packs of cleavers, big wooden spoons, skillets, and cook pots—while a few feet away, out in the rain, Jenny tried to get a fire lit.

Jason meant tried, because the sage she was using was green, and the rain wasn't helping matters. They'd used up the last of their buffalo chips a few days ago, but even that wouldn't have helped. When damp, they were unlightable, and nobody would want to handle them, anyway.

Jason was about to go to her aid when, from across the camp, Megan came out of the rain, bearing a burning torch of twigs beneath her duster, which she held over her back and head and outstretched at arm's length to shelter the flames. He watched as she and Jenny then worked the twigs beneath the pile of brush and brought it to a hissing blaze.

This happened at roughly the same time that various members of the party began to arrive with chickens—one here, two there—already dressed out, and vegetables.

He smiled at the sight of those chickens. Saul Cohen had said that Rachael put her foot down. "If your cooking Olympia and I are going to do, the least you can do is make the food ready, and by that, I mean you should clean it on the inside *and* outside!" she'd announced to the other women.

From that day forward, vegetables had arrived peeled or chopped or washed. Chickens had arrived plucked and gutted, and goats, deer, and antelope had arrived skinned, gutted, and either already on the spit or cleaved into quarters.

Out of respect for Rachael, Olympia requested that no hogs be slaughtered. None were.

For folks that the Reverend Milcher had wanted to leave behind at the side of the road, the Cohens were turning out to be real leading citizens.

Jason was thinking this just as Lavinia Milcher showed up with a pot of sliced carrots and what looked like chopped onions. She stayed on while the other women just dropped off hens or vegetables or bags of flour or cornmeal, and proceeded to fix the dish herself. Jason figured it must be something her kids liked, though

God knows why. When he was a kid, it would have taken the militia to get him to eat carrots.

Rather than being pressed into kitchen duty—Rachael already had Saul cutting up chickens into pieces for frying—Jason walked over to his wagon, leading his palomino mare. Once there, he stripped her of saddle and bridle, and fed her a rasher of oats and barley, topping it off with a handful of corn. While she munched her supper, he walked out through the herd and found his father's roan, Gumption, which he led back to the wagon. He filled Gumption's nose bag with the same mix he'd just fixed for Cleo.

He patted her sleek, golden neck. "Gonna give you the day off tomorrow, Cleo," he said to her before he turned toward Gumption. "'Cause *you're* getting fat." He patted the roan's rump, then climbed up into the wagon.

Jenny was inside, hunched over a book.

"Hello, daredevil," Jason said with a hopeful smile.

She looked up. "Daredevil?"

"Saw you and Megan lighting the fire earlier. Good job."

"Thanks," she replied, without expression, and turned back to her book.

Jason tried again. "What you reading, Jen?"

She held it up, showing him the spine at the same time she said, *"Moby Dick."*

Jason grinned. If she was reading, she was feeling more like herself. Maybe he wouldn't need to leave her off in Santa Fe after all.

Rain pelted the canvas overhead now, and he heard thunder in the distance. He found himself a place to sit, then took off his hat. "Gonna be a goose-drownder."

Jenny said, "A toad-floater."

He grinned back. "We've got to get you started on Jane Austen, Jenny."

She looked up, head cocked. "Why?"

Jason closed his eyes and shrugged. "Just think you ought to be reading some 'girl' books, that's all."

"*What?*"

"Don't holler at me. I'm sleeping. And wake me for supper."

He heard her let out an exasperated groan, but then it was over, just like that. He fell asleep to the sound of raindrops pelting overhead.

14

Three men stood on the banks of the raging creek, now grown to a full-blown river after last night's rain. The rain had stopped hours ago, but it seemed there was no end to the runoff from the Sangre de Cristos.

"They look so far away," Saul Cohen said dreamily.

"Not so far as they did yesterday," added Salmon Kendall.

"Near or far, doesn't matter," said Jason bitterly. So much for his record-making trip to Santa Fe. They could be stuck here for days, and he said so.

"Days, Jason? That long?" Saul asked. "It's moving pretty fast. Seems to me it ought to empty out those mountains in no time."

Salmon shrugged. "Mayhap it's not that deep?"

"Oh, it's deep, all right," Jason said, "and it's running fast. You're right about that, Saul. We'll make camp here, well back from the creek." He turned and pointed farther from the shore, to a line where the grass and brush weren't bent over and slicked with mud. "I don't want anybody closer than ten feet from the other side of that flood line, and have everybody set a rock behind their wheels."

Saul's brows flew up. "The water, it was up here, wasn't it? But that's a good thing, no? See how far it has gone down?"

Salmon shook his head. "Looks to me like it only had

to go down two or three inches to back its way down there, Saul. This here's pretty flat land, where we're standin'."

"What're you bunch of old hens doin'?" came Matt MacDonald's voice from behind them. He was riding up. "Let's get to fordin' that thing." He jabbed his finger toward the swollen banks of the creek.

Jason, as usual, was highly tempted to yank him down off that horse and just plain haul off and slug him. But, also as usual, he held himself back. His back to Matt, he just said, "Can't be done."

"Did you try? Did you even try to ride across?"

"It's very deep, Matthew," said Saul. "He should know, shouldn't he?"

Matt snorted. "Yeah? Well, when was the last time you were through here, Fury? Eight, ten years ago?"

"Six," Jason said.

"Well, a lot of things can change in six years," Matt said. "Hell, that's more than half a decade!" And with that, he goosed his horse into a quick trot, heading straight toward the edge of the water.

Jason hollered, "Hey!"

Saul and Salmon both shouted, "Stop!"

But Matt entered the water, which quickly rose from his horse's fetlocks to knees and hocks. *Any time now,* Jason thought. Then, quite suddenly, it was as if the world had dropped from beneath Matt's horse.

They were both in the rapidly moving creek, with the horse struggling to keep his head above water while Matt tried to stay in the saddle.

"Oh, cripes!" Jason swore softly, then yelled, "Get off! You're drowning him! Get behind him and grab his tail!"

Matt acted as if he were deaf and continued to cling frantically to the horse's back.

"Matt! Matthew MacDonald!" Hamish came thundering up behind Jason and the others. "Jason, get him out of there!"

"Been trying," Jason said. Matt was in the current now, and he and his floundering horse were moving swiftly away. "He won't listen."

"Matt, boy! Can you hear me?" Hamish called. If he could hear, Matt gave no sign. "Dammit, Fury! Do something!"

Jason said, "Give me your horse, Hamish."

Hamish got down and handed over the reins without question.

Jason swung up into the saddle, and took off at a lope, parallel to the swollen creek bed, silently cursing all the while. He knew why he was the one everyone counted on to save this idiot, but wished he'd been at the other end of the forming camp. And then felt guilty for thinking it.

When he came up even with Matt, he pulled Hamish's rope from the horn and shook out a loop. He'd try for the horse's head, but he'd be happy to just get a rope on Matt. The horse could make it out by himself without Matt impeding him.

But his loop snagged the horse's head. He quickly tied the end of it around the horn, and then, praying that Hamish had paid somebody better than he or Matthew to train it, commanded, "Back! Back, old son!"

Lo and behold, the rope grew taut. Matthew's progress was halted, and his horse began to turn in the water, and then slowly began to swim diagonally against the current, toward Jason.

"Good boy. Back, back . . ." Jason kept on talking calmly to Hamish's horse, and the tall gelding kept doing his best to please.

And then Matt's horse began to struggle. Jason knew he was having a hard time kneeing his way over the crest of the bank and carrying Matt's weight, too. So he tried again.

"Matt! Get off him and grab his tail! He'll pull you up right after him!"

Matt shook his head vehemently. Mr. Big Man Matt MacDonald was scared to death, and Jason knew it— and if he didn't get over it pretty damn quick, he was going to get both himself and his horse killed.

"Can I help?" huffed an out-of-breath Hamish, who had apparently run after him.

"Yes," said Jason. He quickly slid down off the horse and told Hamish, "Don't let this horse move until I tell you, got it?"

Hamish gave a quick nod, and Jason took off, running downstream toward Matt and his horse. Once he hit the water, he grabbed the rope to help him keep his balance. He knew that the water would be about waist high on him, unless he went over the invisible bank that Matt's horse was struggling against. He didn't plan to get that far.

Fighting the current, he waded out to about ten feet from the horse's head and called to Matt again. "Get off the damned horse, you fool! He can't make the bank with you on him!"

Nothing. No response.

He walked five feet closer, halving the distance between them. "Matt! Turn your head toward me and look."

Slowly, Matt's head came around. He appeared to see his father, because Jason thought he saw just a touch of relief on his face.

Jason said, "If you're afraid you're going to get kicked, dismount and work your way forward till you can get you hand on the rope, okay?"

This time, Matt nodded. He let go of the reins, much to his horse's relief, and grabbed a handful of wet mane instead. Jason could tell that he'd freed his feet from the stirrups when his backside bobbed to the surface and he began to pull himself forward.

He nearly drowned his horse in the process, but at last he had the rope in his hands and hauled himself forward, hand over hand, to Jason, who said, "You can stand up, now."

Matt did, and seemed surprised when the water was that shallow.

"Get back up to dry land," Jason said. "Tell your father not to let that horse of his move a muscle."

Matt, who was feeling well enough to grumble, threw Jason a sneer and worked his way around him. Jason waited until Matt was halfway back to his father before he moved forward, toward the horse.

He managed to grab one of the reins, snaking along the top of the water, and softly said, "It's all right, old boy. You're safe. Calm down, easy, easy." Slowly, the terrified animal relaxed a bit. Although his hooves still churned the water.

"All right, fella, now this is going to take a little work from both me and you, but we can do it, can't we?" Jason kept on, holding his tone even and light and comforting. "Sure, we can. We won't let that dumbhead be the end of us, will we, boy?"

He snagged the other rein. "All right now, I'm going to let go of this rope. Things are easier when you can breathe, aren't they? And I'm just praying that I won't get swept down in there with you. Now, when I jerk your reins, you just come along with me, just like coming out of a stall that's dug down a mite from constant cleaning, right?"

Jason closed his eyes for a second in silent prayer, then braced himself against the current and let go of the rope. He jerked the reins. "Hup, boy, hup!" he cried.

And the pinto clambered over the crest of the bank, just as easily as a cat running up a tree.

With the horse's bulk to keep him from floating off downstream, Jason threw his arms around the beast's neck. "Good boy!" he cried, then added, more softly, "Atta boy. We weren't going to let that idiot kill us, were we? We're made of tougher stuff than that."

Behind him, on the bank, he heard Hamish applauding and his cries of, "That'a boy, Jason! Good job!"

And then another burst of applause broke out— Saul, Salmon, Dr. Morelli, Megan, Jenny, and a few others had gathered to watch the little drama in the creek.

Jason flushed, grinned, tipped his hat, and began to lead Matt's horse out of the water after he removed the loop he'd tossed over its head. He noticed that the more shallow the water grew, the less the horse shivered—and the more he did.

He shook his head. Jenny would have him smothered in quilts and drinking tea for the rest of the afternoon, if she was truly back to being the old Jenny.

Piled with quilts and grudgingly sipping at the hot tea she'd forced on him, Jason sat silently in the back of the wagon while Jenny sat on the driver's bench, the closed copy of *Moby Dick* beside her.

He was quite the hero, her brother, although he'd never see it that way, let alone admit to it. She was proud of him, truly proud. He had saved Matthew's life. Even Matthew admitted it, and he had more than his share of pride. This she knew. But she couldn't help but admire him, anyway. He had other qualities that more than made up for that tiny shortfall.

Oh, but he looked commanding when he rode that

big spotted gelding of his. And he was handsome, too, handsome as the day was long, with those flashing blue eyes and those cleanly chiseled features and that devilish grin. He'd been so brave to try and ford the creek by himself.

And he was going to be very rich someday. Not that a thing like money mattered to a girl like her, she reminded herself.

But it never hurt, did it?

She wondered . . . If she begged and pleaded with Jason long enough and hard enough, would he leave her behind once they reached their destination?

True, she was only fifteen, but plenty of girls her age were already married and had children.

Which was exactly, although she hardly dared admit it, even to herself, what she was hoping would come about, if she could just figure out how to get Matthew's attention in that way.

She knew that Jason didn't much care for him, and that the feeling was mutual. But then, they were of an age, weren't they? She supposed it was natural for jealousies to arise between them.

Mrs. Matthew MacDonald.

Mrs. Matt MacDonald.

Jenny MacDonald.

Well, a girl could dream, couldn't she?

15

Megan MacDonald carried another pot of coffee to her
wagon, and her brother, the idiot. Honestly, how could
anyone be so blind? And stubborn.

It amazed her that he had lived to see twelve, let
alone twenty. Always doing exactly what he'd been told
not to do, always disobeying orders since the time he
knew what orders were. And he always suffered for it,
which meant that she always had to take care of him in
the aftermath.

She half-wished he'd break his leg or something,
some injury that would keep him immobile and out of
trouble, for a while at least.

But he didn't, so she just kept patching him up and
pouring him coffee and bandaging his blisters. He
wanted to be in charge, he wanted to be the one everyone trusted. He wanted to be Jason.

What he didn't understand was that trust like that
wasn't given, it had to be earned. And Matt did his best
to earn nothing except the occasional sneer. She loved
him, but . . .

After she dropped off the coffee, for which she received little more than a grunt from the still-shivering
and quilt-wrapped Matt, she went to check on his horse.
Jason had stripped him of tack, or maybe it had been
her father, but the gelding still needed a rubdown.
Even in the sunshine, he was shivering.

She went to work on him with a couple of old burlap bags, and soon had him fairly dry and looking a good bit more comfortable. She looked around for Jason's palomino mare, and saw her tied to the Fury wagon, her nose bag on and moving rhythmically with the gentle grinding of grain against molars.

Leave it to Jason to think of his horse first.

Leave it to Matt not to think of his horse at all.

Her smile turned into a scowl. She was embarrassed enough by Matt's actions, but there stood her father, bragging to the Reverend Milcher on his boy's idiocy.

"Rode right out there," Hamish was saying loudly, while he waved his arms about. "Wouldn't take that upstart's word for nothing. Says he would have made it across, too, if Jason had warned him about the current instead of yelling at him to get off his horse. Trying to get my Matthew kicked to death, that's what Jason Fury was up to."

Now, even Megan knew that you should slip off a horse that was going down under you in the water. Slip off and grab his tail, out of reach of those pummeling hooves, and just float along after him. She'd done it herself once, when she was younger and certainly more stupid. And she'd done it out of instinct.

Apparently, Matt couldn't do the right thing even when he had specific instructions.

But then she felt bad. She shouldn't think such things about her only brother, even if he acted like a lunatic half the time.

Well, three quarters.

She turned Matt's horse free and started back toward the wagon. But then she remembered that Matt was in there, and went instead to the Fury wagon. She could use a visit with Jenny.

It didn't hurt that Jason was inside, either.

* * *

"I'd stop with the talking young Fury down, Mr. MacDonald," Saul said as he led his draft horses out to graze.

"Matthew did a foolish thing," he went on. "I know. Wasn't I there? And I think that most of the other people think so, too, and that what Jason did—going out there after him, I mean—was truly brave."

Hamish answered him with a sneer, and then, "Aw, mind your own beeswax, Jew."

Saul said nothing, just gave his head a slow shake and proceeded with the horses. He'd given up on Hamish.

Some had suggested to Saul that oxen would be better for pulling his merchandise wagon, but he liked his Shires. They were sure-footed, very strong, and gave him no trouble. Rachael could drive them all day without incident, and ten-year-old David had no difficulty controlling them, either.

Perhaps Saul would be sorry later on, but at the moment he was glad he didn't have two teams of oxen to deal with. Let alone one. He supposed it would be like having two teams of Hamish MacDonald to contend with each day.

This, he could do without.

"Good for you, Saul," said a voice. It was Salmon Kendall's. He'd led his team of mules and horses out to graze, too. "I overheard what you told MacDonald. He's sure a piece of work, ain't he?"

Two at a time, Saul let his big horses free. The ground practically shook as they trotted away!

"And he reproduced in kind," Saul said, still staring after the Shires.

Salmon laughed loudly as he loosed his mules. "You can sure say that again. Matt's a skunk's behind if ever I met one."

"They're getting set up for dinner," said Saul, who had turned around. He watched his Rachael carrying a bowl of something or other over to Olympia Morelli's cook tent. "I wonder what it will be this evening."

"Sure as hell ain't gonna be nothin' as exotic as pronghorn," Salmon replied. "At least, I ain't been out huntin'. Doubt anybody else has, either."

Saul caught sight of Hamish, leading a party of four men and armed with a big knife: what he'd heard several of the other men refer to as an Arkansas toothpick.

"It will be beef," he said, just as his attention was diverted by the sight of a pretty, young blond woman with a six-year-old girl and a terrier pup tagging at her heels, walking down toward the shoreline. She carried a blanket and a long pole. He pointed. "Isn't that Carrie English?"

"Beef? How do you know? And danged if it ain't, and she's got Chrissy and Rags with her, too."

They watched as she spread out her blanket, sat down on it, summoned Chrissy away from the water's edge, and baited her hook.

"She gonna fish for her dinner?" asked Salmon, as if he'd never seen a woman fish before.

"I believe she is," replied Saul.

Rachael had told him that the petite midwife was running short on supplies already, and it was likely she was trying to keep up her end by supplying a major portion of at least one supper.

He added, "I'll go see, shall I?"

And then, when he'd walked ten feet, it suddenly occurred to him that Salmon had lost his wife, and just recently. It wouldn't hurt for Salmon to go help a pretty widow, would it?

"Salmon!" he called. "Hey, Salmon!"

And as Salmon turned around and approached him, he thought, *Better her than the Widow Jameson, at least.*

* * *

Eulaylee Jameson and her daughter, Cynthia—just as plain, dark, and beetle-browed as her mother—were, at that moment, carrying a basket of canned goods to the cook tent. There were home-canned tomatoes and peas and potatoes in this haul. Yesterday had been strawberry preserves, apricot jelly, and enough dried apples for three pies.

Eulaylee, Cynthia believed, was getting more than a little sick and tired of this community cooking business. The way Eulaylee would see it, her preserves were hers, period. According to her mother, nobody could cook or can as well as she could, anyway, so why should she be forced to share with a bunch of people who didn't know which end of the ham to keep for yourself, and which one to send to the church poor drive?

"Philistines," Eulaylee muttered under her breath.

"Yes, Mama," said the long-suffering Cynthia. She didn't have much more charm than her mother, but she was at least relieved that somebody else was doing the cooking without demanding that she be pressed into service.

Her sister, Deborah, had been in a state ever since the men brought her back from the Comanche camp, and their mother was doing nothing to make things any better. To hear their mother tell it, you'd think that Deborah had held up her arms and said, "Take me!"

And their brother was no help, either. A mama's boy to the end, Elmer was the one who'd planted the idea that Debby has been a more than willing captive.

The peckerwood.

Sometimes, she'd just like to punch him. Except that wouldn't be very ladylike, would it? Cynthia was constantly concerned about being a lady. After all, she was practically an old maid, and she'd thought that perhaps she could find herself a man on the trip west.

So far, she wasn't having much luck. Jason Fury and Matt MacDonald were too young, although they were both highly attractive. Hamish MacDonald was too old and too gruff and reminded her too much of her mother.

Salmon Kendall and Randall Nordstrom had both lost their wives in the Comanche attack and were both of about the right age, but she didn't think it would be proper to single one of them out quite yet.

She'd give it another week or two, although her mother had been nudging her toward Randall Nordstrom since the very day they shoveled the first grave dirt over his poor wife.

And then there were the hired men. But somehow, Cynthia felt she was a little above Milt Billings and Ward Wanamaker and Gil Collins, even though she found herself fascinated by Gil. He had such nice blond hair and such a clean, straight nose. . . .

"Cynthia! Honestly, girl. Get your head out of the clouds!" her mother snapped. They were at the cook tent already, and she helped her mother swing the basket of preserves up onto the table.

Olympia Morelli—who was getting far too big to be decently out in public, Cynthia thought—took the jars from their basket, thanking them effusively for each one. That Jewish woman was there, too, and smiled at her.

Cynthia looked away, embarrassed to be noticed.

Her mother had refused to eat any supper the first couple of nights that Rachael Cohen helped with the cooking, but all those good smells finally got to her. She finally ate. But she still wouldn't admit it was any good, even though Cynthia had caught her scraping her plate more than once.

"Roast beef tonight, Mrs. Jameson," a smiling Olympia Morelli said to Cynthia's mother. "Mr. MacDonald is slaughtering a steer. Your tomatoes, peas, and potatoes will make wonderful side dishes."

Eulaylee grunted a response, then abruptly turned and walked back toward her wagon. Cynthia curtsied, said, "Thank you, I'm sure," to Mrs. Morelli, and trotted to catch up.

Eulaylee glanced up the bank, then froze. Cynthia nearly ran into her.

"Well, would you take a look at that!"

Cynthia followed her mother's pointing finger to the figures on the creek's bank, about a hundred yards away.

"Why, I believe that's Salmon Kendall with Carrie English! And his wife's not dead a fortnight!"

Actually it had been more than three weeks, but Cynthia knew better than to open her mouth.

"Why don't you have Salmon Kendall following you around?" her mother wanted to know.

"I didn't think it was proper to—"

"Proper, my bustle! Well, it's probably too late now. You're going to stay an old maid all of your life, Cynthia Ann Jameson, unless you start baiting your line for Randall Nordstrom! He's probably a better catch anyway."

They had reached their wagon.

Eulaylee climbed up first, wagging her large backside at a frowning Cynthia, who followed, muttering, "Yes, Mama."

16

It was ten in the morning before Milt and Ward rode back into camp with the news that although the water had significantly retreated, there wasn't a decent place for fording within miles. Ward's horse was covered with drying mud up to his belly, and Milt reported that the meadowland on either side of the creek was all in the same condition—waterlogged.

For the first time, Jason was at a loss. The main part of the creek bed itself was probably eight to ten feet deep with a sharp drop-off on either side, worn that way by all the rainstorms since he'd last been through with his father. There was barely a trickle of water going through it today, although a few muddy sinkholes existed where large carp, washed down from somewhere upstream, gasped their last.

"What you thinkin', Jason?" Ward asked. "Build a bridge?"

Jason smiled momentarily. "Out of what?"

Ward looked around at the featureless landscape and gave a sheepish grin. "Oh, yeah."

But then Jason recalled a story his father had told him, about taking a train of settlers out to Oregon, in which he was faced with a similar problem. Jason said, "On the other hand, Ward, you may not be far from wrong."

"Huh?" Ward scratched the back of his head, bobbing his hat up and down.

"You feel like digging?"

Ward's nose wrinkled. "I must be feeble, Jason, 'cause I don't know what in tarnation you're talkin' about."

Jason said, "You will, Ward. You will."

By two in the afternoon, Jason had put together two gangs of men for the work.

Hamish MacDonald wasn't happy.

"If I wanted to wreck my pants and boots, I could've just stayed home and dangled 'em in the creek," Matt said as he slipped into his oldest trousers.

"That blasted Jason Fury," Hamish grumbled. "This whole thing is his fault. I saw a map. We could have swung farther south and crossed the Canadian River all at once, but nay, we have to ford every bloody branch of it. And what kind of fool calls a river 'the Canadian' this bloody far from Canada, anyway? We're practically in Mexico!"

Matthew jerked a boot on. "Damned if I know," he said without expression.

"And now that little brat of a lad has us *digging* our way out! Might as well try digging to China, I say!" Hamish grabbed a shovel and tossed it to Matt, then grabbed the other one for himself.

"Tell him, then, Pa. Or tell your friend Milcher. I already know how you feel about it."

Hamish glowered at his son good and hard, but those parental glowers didn't work like they used to. Honestly, he didn't know what was going on with his son. Or the world in general, it seemed.

Digging! Manual labor. The hired men should be doing this, not every man in the bloody camp.

It offended Hamish's entire sense of class structure. "Pa?"

He turned toward Matthew. "What?"

"This time, aren't you the one putting on a little too much of the English?"

Before he realized it, Hamish did something that he had often had the inclination to do, but never had. He slapped his son across the face, just as hard as he could.

"Sass!" he roared as Matthew picked himself up off the floor of the wagon. "You're as bad as Jason Fury, sassing your betters."

Matthew, his cheek red with the imprints of his father's fingers and palm, merely smiled. Which only made Hamish madder.

"I don't know what this world is coming to." Hamish climbed down out of the wagon, leaving his ungrateful son to his own devices.

By three in the afternoon, the two teams of men had dug down the near slope of the bank. Jason had them start well back at a narrow angle, digging their shovels into the sodden earth and emptying them down into the creek itself.

By the time they pitched the last shovelfuls down into the creek, the earth they'd uncovered was dry and the creek bed was a quarter filled with earth.

Then they started on the walls of the opposite bank, digging down the muddy waterway and casting the refuse at their feet. Jason planned for them to dig the path two wagons wide, and on a shallow slope both down and up, filling the creek itself halfway to the top of its original bank.

Things were going along quite handily, too, aside from the grumbling from Hamish and Matt MacDonald, when he heard sounds approaching from the way they had come.

"Everybody, get your guns. Get back to the wagons and your families." It didn't sound like marauding Indians, but it could very easily be brigands and thieves. They were driving wagons. At least, it sounded like they were.

He had only reached his own wagon when they came into sight: a wagon train, just like theirs. It was somewhat smaller and battered. Some of the wagon canvases showed signs of burning and they had no herd or remuda.

Jason, his rifle over his shoulder, jumped down from his wagon and walked forward, holding up a hand. The incoming wagons stopped, and a middle-aged fellow, his greying head bandaged and one arm in a sling, rode out to meet him.

"Had some trouble?" Jason asked.

"Comanche," the wounded man said. "They killed nigh on half of us—men, women, kids, it didn't matter—before they ran off our herd. We're half-starved, mister. Best we've done since the attack was a deer, three days back."

"Well, settle your wagons here, friend. We'll feed you, and we've got a doctor, too."

"Bless you, son, may God bless you all," came the broken-voiced reply. Jason could see tears brimming in the man's eyes. "What are you called, son?"

"I'm sorry," Jason said. "I'm Jason Fury, sir."

"Well, by God." The man took off his hat and slapped it across his heart. "You any relation to my good friend Jedediah Fury?"

"His son, sir."

The man let out a happy hoot. "He here, or are you leadin' this whole shebang by your lonesome? Oh, and

I'm Colorado Gooding, leadin' what's left of this tattery crew to Santa Fe."

"I've heard my father speak of you, Mr. Gooding," Jason said, and held up his hand, which Gooding shook. "But I have bad news. My father was killed on the trail a few weeks back. Comanche, possibly the same band that attacked you."

"Lordy," breathed Gooding as he bowed his head. "Ain't nothin' good in the world anymore? The great Jedediah Fury, dead and gone."

Jason suddenly realized that he felt much the same. There had been so much to take care of, so many people to handle and manage, that he hadn't had time to mourn. He hadn't thought he needed to. But right now, in the presence of this stranger, he found himself crying just like a kid.

He wiped his eyes with his shirt sleeve, but that didn't stop the tears from falling. Before he realized what was happening, Colorado Gooding had dismounted.

"We're all gonna miss him terrible, son," Gooding said, and he was crying now, too. "Somethin' terrible."

Jason didn't know how long they stood there, in the middle of that meadow, weeping. All he knew was that when it was done, he felt better. And he was pretty damned glad that Hamish and Matt MacDonald hadn't been there to see him.

"Sorry," he said as he finally backed up and stood erect. He gave a final wipe to his eyes. "Didn't mean to go all blubbery on you, Mr. Gooding. My pa always taught me that men don't cry."

Gooding actually chuckled and sniffled at the same time. "Well, Jason, even your pa couldn't be right about everything. And call me Colorado. Now tell me. What are you folks doin' stopped out here on a nice day like this?"

*   *   *

They moved Gooding's wagons around half of Jason's, in a semicircle, and then Jason showed Gooding the dig. Gooding immediately added what few able-bodied men he had left to the project, and then sent the others to Dr. Morelli, who was obviously thrilled to be able to put down his shovel and pick up instruments more suitable to his profession.

The digging was finished by nightfall, and once again, the men butchered a steer and the womenfolk put together a meal. Gooding's people ate ravenously.

Jason, Saul, Morelli, Salmon, Hamish, Colorado Gooding, and a few of Colorado's men all sat near the main campfire, eating good barbecued beef, hot corn bread with butter and jelly, and a variety of canned vegetables from practically every wagon in Jason's train.

"You sure it was Comanche?" Hamish was asking.

"Sure as the day I was borned," Colorado replied. "Filty bastards."

"I wonder why they let us off so easy," Hamish mused as he helped himself to more coffee.

"I'd hardly call it 'easy,'" Jason said. "And we had quite a few more men with guns."

"That knew how to use them, anyway," Colorado said with a shake of his head. "We was damned lucky to keep our scalps."

One of his men, a big Swede called Thorson, nodded in agreement. "We are lucky to be eating this good meal with you, to have lived this long. I lost my brother and his wife, and even I took a spear in my leg."

"Lucky I caught it when I did, Thorson," said Dr. Morelli. "You were pretty close to gangrene."

"Didn't your people have a doctor in their number?" Saul asked in amazement. "Or sugar cubes?"

Colorado blinked, then shook his head. "Closest we had to a doc was a midwife. But she got killed right off. And what's sugar cubes got to do with anything?"

Jason said, "Long story, Colorado."

"You say you knew Jason's papa?" Hamish asked.

"Me an' ol' Jedediah Fury go way back to forty-nine," Colorado replied. "You know, when everybody and his brother went gold-crazy? Why, practical every other feller in the country was off to see the elephant, and it was folks like me and Jedediah what took 'em there."

"Elephants? There are elephants where we are going?" Saul asked, his eyes wide.

Salmon, sitting next to him, whispered, "Not really. I'll tell you later."

"More than once, me and Jedediah met up somewhere and hooked our caravans together," Colorado went on. "Strength in numbers and all that. By God, this is fine beef, Jason. My regards to the cook."

"Cooks," Jason corrected him, catching Megan's eye.

"In fact, I was thinking—if Jason ain't got no objections—that mayhap we could tag along with you as far as Santa Fe."

"That where you're headed, then, is it?" Hamish asked.

"Yup. All right with you, Jason?"

"Fine by me," Jason said.

17

The two trains, now one, crossed the creek the next morning, saving the Widow Griggs, whose late husband, Milton, had installed a cast-iron bottom in his wagon, and had carried an anvil in it, for last, right before the livestock were run across.

By the time the last goat bleated its way across, water was already beginning to seep across the lowest part of the built-up, artificial path they'd made to bridge the creek. Jason knew, because he stayed behind, watching to make certain that every single wagon, ox, horse, cow, pig, goat, and dog made it across without problem.

Colorado Gooding was somewhere up front, he supposed, taking much pleasure in heading up such a large train of wagons. And Hamish MacDonald was probably right beside him, talking up the beauties of the lands beyond Santa Fe, at least what he'd heard or read about them.

Jason reined Cleo around and loped her up past the herd to catch up with the wagons. People actually looked happy this morning, where they had appeared sharp or cross or simply dejected before. Maybe it was because they were finally moving again. Maybe it was because the rain was over, and the sky was clear.

Whatever the reason, he was just thankful. Even Eulaylee Jameson, her cat, Boots, dozing in her lap, waved and smiled when he passed her rig. He was so surprised, in fact, that it took him a second to return the gesture and add, "Fine morning, isn't it, Mrs. Jameson?"

"Lovely, Mr. Fury, just lovely," she replied with a genuine grin before she turned her attention back to her team.

Jason dug his heels into his mare before Eulaylee had a chance to think of any other questions, but slowed down when he reached the Cohens' rigs. Saul was driving the one behind, the rig that carried the merchandise for his hardware store.

"Mornin'," Jason called.

Saul waved. "Nice day, isn't it?"

"That why everybody's in such a good mood?"

Saul said, "I believe so. This troubles you?"

Jason thumbed his hat back. "Only insofar as Eulaylee Jameson smiled at me, Saul."

Saul laughed. "I supposed that might trouble me as well, but then, I have the safety of my Rachael's skirts to hide behind, don't I?" He wiggled his eyebrows comically. "And I am not such a fine figure of a man as you, Jason. Rachael says you make all the girls' hearts beat a little faster."

Jason made a face and waved his hand at Saul. "These women don't have enough to do that they've got to gossip all day?"

Saul said "We men brag about the animals we hunt or the men we best." Saul shrugged. "Maybe it gives them something to do while they cook. While they do the things that women do." The grin faded from his face, and he said, "Jason, you watch out for that Alabama man."

"Who?"

"Montana. Utah. Whatever his name is."

"Colorado?"

Saul nodded.

"Why? He was a friend of my pa's, Saul."

Saul shook his head, then said, "Something bothers me. Perhaps it is just that he is too friendly with Hamish and the reverend. Perhaps it is only that I do not believe he has bathed in too long a time. I don't know. Don't listen to me."

"No, Saul, no," Jason said. "I've been concerned about Colorado, myself." He didn't say how much. All he knew was that he wasn't going to go suspecting the man he'd blubbered all over last night of . . . what? Commandeering his wagon train? That was just crazy.

Still, he waved Saul good-bye and goosed his mare ahead, toward the front of the train. It was getting on toward afternoon, and he'd best be up front when Hamish found out there was another branch of the creek to ford.

It looked to him like Colorado Gooding had added nine wagons to their force. Most were driven by women, but he saw a few strange men on horseback. To these, he rode up and introduced himself.

He met Paul Hartung, Garth Witherspoon, Mel Sanderson, farmers and ranchers all, and Raul Chavez, a native of Santa Fe, who had ridden all the way to Kansas City to pick out new pigments for his stained-glass business, and was now hauling them back with Gooding's caravan.

"The other hombres, they were killed by Comanche," he said, in a thick Mexican accent. "My own brother, Luis, was among the dead."

Jason nodded. "I guess we've all lost somebody."

"Mr. Gooding, he tells us of your father. I am sorry, amigo."

"Thanks. Sorry for your brother, too. Were you two in the glass business together?"

"*Sí.* He was learning the trade." Chavez suddenly looked ahead, staring. "*Dios mio.* Is this yet another creek to be forded?"

"Probably," muttered Jason. He tipped his hat and loped on ahead, leaving Chavez behind.

"Damn it!" Hamish roared. He was off his horse and pounding his thigh with his fisted hat. "Damn it, I knew it."

Jason figured there had been quite a bit of swearing that came before, and was glad that he had only just ridden up. He, too, dismounted.

He looked down, and said, "Well, it looks like we've got another hole to start filling, Hamish."

Colorado burst into laughter while Hamish grumbled. The Reverend Milcher, who had ridden a few feet off to the side, probably so as not to sully his ears with Hamish's profanity, rode closer and stopped.

"Dear Lord," he muttered, just loud enough to be heard.

"There you be right on the money, Reverend," cackled Colorado.

Hamish turned an irate face toward Jason. "If you'd done the sensible thing and taken us farther south, we would've only had to ford this bloody thing one blasted time."

Actually, it would have been twice, but Jason wasn't about to quibble. He was more inclined to punch Hamish right in the middle of his furry red face. But he didn't. He stood his ground and clenched and unclenched his jaw, and then said, "Hamish, if you don't want to dig, then why don't you take a couple of men and go shoot us a couple of deer or antelope for supper?"

Hamish gritted his teeth and swung back up on his horse and, without a word, rode back along the line of wagons toward the remuda. Jason noticed that he pulled his boy out of line to follow him.

Good riddance, Jason thought, and turned his attention back to the gaping hole that ran the length of the creek bed.

This branch carried quite a bit more water than the previous passage, and was wider and deeper. The banks were only six or seven feet above the water, although there was no telling how deep that water was. Not without going in.

With a sigh, he tossed his reins to Colorado, who said, "Hope you can swim, boy."

Jason looked up. "You want to volunteer?"

Colorado waved his arms. "Wouldn't dream of robbin' you of the pleasure."

Muttering, "I didn't think so," Jason walked to the edge of the bank and slid straight down it, on his butt. Upon landing, he found himself knee-deep in water, and called up, "You'd best toss me down a loop, Colorado, or I'll never get back up."

In a matter of seconds, a rope sailed down and landed in front of him in the brown murk. He picked it up and waded out to the middle, then the opposite bank, then ten feet upstream and back across. The water, at its deepest, was only waist-high on him—a depth that, under normal circumstances, could be easily forded by both livestock and wagons. The bed was gravel and seemed solid enough. The problem would be getting the wagons and livestock down to it.

Well, it wasn't like he was new to digging.

He snugged the rope around his middle, sloshed back down to where the horses were waiting above, took a steady grip on the rope, and cried, "Start hauling, Colorado!"

*   *   *

The second dig wasn't as bad as the first.

For one thing, they had a few more men on the crew, right from the start. For another, all the dirt could be thrown to the side instead of carried to, and thrown into, the creek itself. Still, it took them until well after dark, and they were not finished, even then.

Jason called a halt for the day, and they all trooped back to the now-circled wagons and the cook fire.

Dinner was a little sparse, Jenny thought. Hamish, Matt, and their men hadn't been able to scare up more than one thin buck for their dinner, but the women had stretched it by making venison stew with plenty of home-canned okra, peas, potatoes, onions, and tomatoes. And one of the Cohen's goats. The goat's name was Nellie, and Jenny was sorry to see her butchered.

Saul sat next to Jason and Jenny while they ate, his wife having taken charge of the children, and every once in a while, tired though he was, he said, "Well, now, I believe that was a piece of my Nellie. Not so gamy, you know?"

And Jason would laugh through his fatigue, Jenny would smile, and Saul would shrug his shoulders.

And they all would think very unkind thoughts about Hamish and Matt MacDonald. Except for Jenny. She was still thinking kind thoughts about Matt. More than kind, as a matter of fact.

Just that morning, he had kissed her behind the shelter of his father's wagon. There was no particular reason for it, which made it all the more exciting for Jenny. He had simply led his horse up to her, after Megan, to whom she'd been talking, went up front. He grabbed a pair of gloves out of the back of the wagon, smiled, leaned over, kissed her square on the mouth, mounted up, and rode off.

All without a word.

She'd been thinking about it all day long. And she

hadn't told anyone, not even Megan. Not even her diary. And especially not Jason.

Jason would throw a fit, wouldn't he?

Especially now, as exhausted as he was. He was practically falling asleep while he ate, although she had been able to coax him into changing out of those muddy clothes. That was something, anyway. Usually, she couldn't get him to do anything that was even halfway good for him.

But even now, tired and dirty, he was still remarkably handsome, she thought. If she'd been an artist or a sculptor, she couldn't think of any other subject she'd rather paint or model than her brother. Or Matthew MacDonald. Either one would do quite beautifully.

She realized that the little group had gone silent, and looked over at Jason and Saul. Saul had fallen back against the wagon's wheel, and was asleep with his mouth open. Jason dozed with his chin on his chest.

"Some wagon master," she muttered, and stood up to step over her brother. She put her hand gently on Saul's shoulder, and when he opened one eye, said, "It's time to go to your wagon, Mr. Cohen."

As she helped him to his feet, she heard a distant rumble of thunder and muttered, "Wonderful. Just what we need."

When Saul had sleepily stumbled off a good twenty feet and his wife came out to make sure he got all the way home, Jenny bent to Jason.

She had him, in fact, clear up into the wagon and had his boots pried off before the skies opened.

18

Jenny didn't know how she'd fallen asleep. But she must have, for the next thing she knew Jason was gone and there was a lot of yelling outside, mixed in with the battering of rain on the lightning-brightened canvas roof.

Quickly, she poked her head outside. She might as well have poured a bucket of water over her head, the rain was that fast and thick. But through it, she was able to see men rushing from their wagons and toward the creek. Mr. Kendall was going from wagon to wagon, right around the circle, waking them up, and it wasn't long before he came to hers.

He was trotting through the mud, going to go right on past, but she flagged him down. "Mr. Kendall! What is it? What's wrong?"

He looked wild-eyed. "It's Carrie English! Her wagon's goin' in the creek!" He was off and running again before the last words were out of his mouth.

After glancing back to make certain that Jason had heard, too, Jenny jumped down from the wagon without thinking about a coat or hat, even in the cold rain, and began slogging her way toward the creek. She couldn't imagine why the Widow English had moved her wagon so near the stream that it could slide in. It had been a good thirty feet from the bank this afternoon, while the men were digging.

Jenny picked up her pace. There was little Chrissy to think of, and Rags.

Carrie English, soaked and sobbing, was now sheltered in Hamish MacDonald's comforting grip, and the last thing Jason heard, when he ran for his horse, was Hamish saying, "Don't you worry, lass, Jason'll get her."

He prayed that Hamish was, for once, right. He leapt into Cleo's saddle—which had been put in place by Ward—and loped along the water's edge, signaling Ward and Saul and Morelli to get a move on, too. It was black as pitch, save for the lightning that flashed all too near, and he felt as though he were standing in a shower bath. A cold one.

But as he neared the wagon, floating downstream in the current, he pulled his rope off the horn, tethered one end of it there, and leapt down off Cleo's back, carrying the rest of the coil.

"You know what to do!" he called to Ward before he waded out into the current, letting out rope as he moved closer to the wagon.

Ward nodded at him, and that was the last time he looked back.

The wagon was still floating, but he didn't know how much longer that piece of luck would hold out. And he mentally kicked himself for the thousandth time. He should have reminded Carrie to block the wheels of her wagon. Hell, he should have blocked them himself. Her wagon had been well up from the water's edge, but on a slight incline.

But who could have known it would rain so blasted much and so hard? Who could have known the water would rise so fast, and that the ground beneath the wagons would turn to slick, slippery mud?

He should have, that was who.

The water, having gone from ankle- to thigh-high, was suddenly over his head. He fought to pull himself to the surface—and also, to remember to hang onto that rope. Just as he thought his lungs would burst, his head cleared the water. He began to swim for the wagon, aided by the current, and finally grabbed the driver's bench with one hand. He heard a cheer go up behind him, on the bank, but didn't look back. He wasn't done yet.

He quickly looped the rest of the rope around the bench, tying it off hard, while he shouted, "Chrissy? Chrissy, you in there?"

A tiny, drowsy voice answered, "Yessir?"

Wasn't that just like a little kid, to sleep through something like this?

"You just hold still, baby," he shouted before he turned back to Ward. "Toss me another!" he called.

Ward's loop sailed out and just about settled over Jason's head. It would have, too, if he hadn't shot a hand out to catch it. This one, he tied to the whiffle bar, diving underwater to do so. When he came up, Saul was ready for him. Just like that, another loop rocketed out from the bank. It landed on top of the driver's bench, which he tied it round.

He signaled the men, and one by one, the ropes went taut and the wagon stopped moving. Thank God. A glance over his shoulder showed him that Morelli had switched horses, and was sitting on Cleo now, holding her steady.

Then, at last, Jason said, "Chrissy, honey, come here. We're gonna take a little swim."

Her head popped up and she blinked. "Is that you, Mr. Fury?"

He nodded and held out a hand. "Come on, baby."

"Where's Rags?"

The dog. He hadn't seen hide nor hair of it. He said,

"He went on ahead of us, Chrissy. He's all right." He hoped to hell it wasn't a lie.

At last, he felt the little girl put her tiny hand in his.

Rags had indeed jumped from the wagon, but swum the wrong way. Now he was a hundred feet downstream from the wagon, swimming desperately for the bank.

Jenny kept pace with him, encouraging him. "Good boy, Rags! You can do it." She had run past Jason, who had already been tying the first rope on the wagon seat. There was nothing she could do there. But she'd heard a faint, terrified yip from downstream, and had followed the sound.

Her skirts felt like lead, weighing her down, holding her back, and she stopped to strip out of them. Nobody would see her clear down here.

Rushing ahead in nothing but her chemise and pantaloons, she splashed into the muddy water. Rags was tiring, she could see it. He'd stopped barking, and was now stroking only intermittently.

"Rags!" she shouted. "Don't you dare die! What will Chrissy do without you?"

The water was up to her waist, but she kept moving forward. For not the first time, she blessed her papa for throwing her into Folger's Creek one spring afternoon, long ago. Her mother had been fit to be tied, but she'd learned how to swim. Even if she had got her new Easter dress soaked through.

A few more steps and she reached the drop-off. She went under the surface, but unburdened by a rope and guns and heavy boots, she bobbed right up to the surface, blinked muddy water from her eyes, and began to swim for the now-limp puppy.

* * *

Jason made his way slowly up one of the ropes, with Chrissy clinging to his neck, and giggling. He was glad somebody was enjoying this.

As he pulled his way toward the bank, which seemed a lot farther off when he was trying to get to it than when he'd swum out to the wagon, the men on the ropes slowly backed their horses, helping him a little.

"Mr. Fury, I don't see Rags," came Chrissy's voice. "Where is he?"

"Let's worry about Rags later, all right, sugar?" he said, just as he felt his boot touch the bank. He stepped up on its spongy surface, and was suddenly in water that was only hip-deep. Ward whistled his admiration, and Saul and Dr. Morelli both broke out in big grins.

As Jason shifted the little girl into one arm, he wished he could be as happy as they seemed. They might haul that wagon a piece, but sure as anything, the tongue was going to sink in and stick it, and keep it stuck.

At last, Jenny reached the pup and latched onto him, pulling him toward her. He let out a weak yelp, letting her know he was still alive. His curly coat, usually black, tan, and white, was now a sodden, solid, dirty brown from the water, and his usually hard, muscled body felt like a dishrag.

Still, she clasped him to her and began to stroke, one-armed, for the bank. Progress was slow, and she feared she was far from the wagons by this time. She was tiring, too, and each pull toward the creek's edge took more and more out of her.

She began to wonder if she'd ever set her feet on the earth again.

One stroke. Another. The bank seemed just as far away.

And then she felt something, something wet, but warm. Rags, licking her cheek. "We'll make it, boy," she whispered, and got a mouthful of water for her trouble.

And then she heard a faint whistling sound, and a *plop*.

And Matt's voice. "Put it around you, Jenny!"

Suddenly, she realized what he was talking about. His rope floated only a few feet from her. She stroked again, and managed to get her hand on it, then her wrist through the loop. She hung on for all she was worth.

"Got it!" she shouted weakly.

The rope began to pull her toward shore with what seemed like magical swiftness.

"Let go of the damned dog and grab it with both hands!" Matt yelled. "I'm gonna pull your arm off!"

"Just keep going," Jenny called back, and tightened her grip on the puppy.

Matt said something she couldn't make out, but he kept pulling. And he was right. By the time she made the bank and was able to stand up, her arm felt as if it had been wrenched from its socket.

"You all right?" Matt asked, once she had walked clear of the water. "You're naked!"

"I'm fine, thank you, and I am *not* naked! I have my underwear on."

He said, "Could'a fooled me."

She looked down at herself just as the lightning flashed overhead. The water had made the cotton of her underthings clinging and nearly transparent. In shock and shame, she figured that at least he couldn't look at her if she was behind him.

She shifted the puppy to her bad arm and held the other up to Matt. "Give me a ride back to my clothes, please."

Matt reached down and hauled her up behind his

saddle. "Real shame, if you ask me," he said, then clucked to his horse.

And despite herself, Jenny felt a strange and not un-welcome tingle zipper its way up her spine.

Chrissy having been delivered into the hands of Dr. Morelli, Jason took the last rope and prepared himself to go back into the water.

"What are you *doing*?" Saul asked, over the thunder.

"Gonna dive down and hook up the tongue," Jason said. The wagon's tongue was the pole that came off the whiffle bar and extended up, between the two pairs of horses that pulled the wagon. And it was stuck in the creek's bed already. They had made no further progress on getting the wagon out.

Ward hopped off his horse. "Lemme go this time, Jason."

Jason shook his head. "I need you out here, Ward, holding pressure on the wagon."

"But—"

"Doc, give me your rope, and snug up the other end around your saddle horn."

Morelli hesitated a moment, but then did as he was told. Jason tossed him one end of the rope, uncoiled several loops to give him sufficient slack, and then waded in.

When he made his way to the wagon's bench, he took a deep breath before he dove down. He knew he wouldn't be able to see anything, so he felt his way down to the whiffle, then along the tongue until he found the clos-est ring to the end.

Quickly, he threaded the rope through it, but ran out of air before he could tie it off.

He broke the surface gasping and sputtering, but before he could dive down again, he heard Saul call out, "Tie it there, Jason! Tie it at the surface!"

At first, he thought Saul was crazy, but then he realized that the end going to the saddle horn was taut. "Right!" he called back, and pulled on the other end of the rope until it, too, was taut. He pulled so hard, in fact, that he felt the wagon's tongue come free from the creek's bed.

"Hold that horse still," he shouted to Saul, and kept on pulling until the end of the tongue broke the water's surface. Then and only then did he tie it off, at the ring, then turn for shore to the shouts of the men and the giggles of a little girl, who was having the time of her life.

He made it out of the water just as that terrier pup of Chrissy's came galloping up the side of the creek, barking and yapping and carrying on. He looked like he hadn't had such a happy time of it, but he was delighted to hear the little girl's laughter.

"Rags!" she cried gleefully. "Rags! Mr. Fury, you were right!" Morelli let her slide to the ground, and the pup flew into her arms.

"I'll be danged!" Ward muttered.

"Miracles happen all around us," said Saul, with a shake of his head.

"All right, everybody," said Jason as he swung up on Dr. Morelli's horse. The battering rain was punishing them all. "We don't have this rig out of the soup yet."

19

The next morning found the men digging again—or at least as much as they could, the water still being high—most of the women washing out muddy clothes, and Carrie English's belongings all sitting out in the sun to dry.

As for Carrie, she was grateful. Grateful her child had been saved—which she was told was due to Jason Fury in its entirety—grateful her possessions were only damp, not lost forever, and grateful that her daughter's only companion, a little terrier mix, had survived.

Matt MacDonald had told her she had Jenny Fury to thank for that. He'd said she'd swum right out, brave as you please, caught the floundering dog, and brought it safely to shore.

She wondered if he was sweet on Jenny. Of course, he was the only man, outside of her brother, who was of a suitable age for Jenny. What was she? Fifteen? Sixteen? And she certainly was pretty. She had her brother's wheat-blond hair and good looks and elegant carriage.

And his good heart, it seemed.

Carrie hoped the creek wouldn't go down too fast. After all, some of her things were still dripping. Her mother's breakfront was going to be all right, too, she thought with a sigh of relief. It had been her grand-mother's before that, and had made the trip, by sailing ship, all the way across the ocean from Ireland. A great many hopes and dreams were tied up in that old piece of furniture.

Rags ran past her, followed by Chrissy.

"Mr. Kendall's coming, Mama," Chrissy said as she went by.

Instinctively, Carrie's hand went to her hair, to straighten it.

"All right, baby. Go play," Carrie said.

Jenny sneezed again, and snuggled down farther into her quilts. After all, hadn't Dr. Morelli told her to stay in bed today? He hadn't said she couldn't read, though, and *Moby Dick* was under her pillow.

But somehow, she found she couldn't concentrate on Captain Ahab and Starbuck or the great white whale this morning. All she could think about was Matthew MacDonald.

She loved him, and she couldn't tell a soul, although she was bursting to.

There was a knock on the wagon's tailgate, and then Megan's head appeared above it. Megan said, "Morning!"

Jenny said, "You'd best keep your distance. Dr. Morelli thinks I'm getting a cold. You know, from last night."

"We all ought to have one, then," Megan replied. "I've never been so cold and wet in all my born days."

Jenny couldn't stand it anymore. And Megan wouldn't tell, would she? She said, "Megan, I have something to tell you. But you've got to promise that you won't tell a living soul, that you'll take it to your grave!"

Megan cocked a brow. "Well, that sounds important!"

"It's the most important thing I've ever had to say in my whole live-long life!"

Megan sat down and leaned forward. "Well, I promise then. Cross my heart and hope to die."

"Megan, I . . . I'm in love with your brother." There. It was out.

Megan blinked, but otherwise there was no change in her expression.

A scowl came over Jenny's face. She had expected quite a bit more than that! "What?" she demanded.

"Jenny, you're my very best friend, and I love my brother, but . . ."

"But?"

"But I don't think he's the kind you ought to fall in love with, that's all."

Jenny's hands twisted her quilt. "And just what kind is that?"

"Morning, ma'am," Salmon Kendall said with a tip of his hat.

"Won't you sit down, Salmon?" Carrie replied, pointing to a barrel set out to dry.

Salmon sat, looking generally nervous, and took off his hat. He passed its brim, over and over again, through his long fingers.

Carrie waited and waited, and finally broke the silence. "And what can I do for you this morning, Salmon?"

"Nothin'," he said, then quickly added, "Well, quite a bit."

"Yes?" she urged.

"Well, it's just that last night, when you . . . you know . . . I got to thinkin' 'bout . . ." Suddenly, he stood straight up. "I . . . I gotta go." He slapped his hat back on his head and turned on his heel.

Carrie watched after him. If he wasn't a man with marriage on his mind, she'd eat her hat. Maybe his, too. But she wondered if it was her he really wanted, or just another woman to take his wife's place. It was very soon, she realized. Perhaps too soon.

She would wait and see.

Megan hopped down from the Fury wagon, feeling terrible. She was a traitor to her brother and a traitor to her best friend, all at once. To her brother, because she should have stood up for him instead of talking him down—even though he deserved it—and to Jenny, because her feelings were real and true, and Megan had dashed her tender hopes.

Or at least, she thought she had. Hoped she had. And hoped she hadn't.

She walked back to her own wagon, then changed her mind before she reached it, altering her path to take her down by the creek. Jason would be there. It did her good just to look at him. Maybe, if she stared at him long enough, she could think what to do.

When she reached the creek, Abigail Krimp had a blanket all laid out, and invited Megan to join her. Megan was grateful for the chance at a dry perch.

Abigail proved a little too chatty, though.

Mostly, about Jason.

"Isn't he just the handsomest thing?" Abigail said, so close to a swoon that Megan was embarrassed for her.

"Who?" she asked, although there could be little doubt about whom Abigail had spoken. She was staring straight at Jason.

"Mr. Fury, of course!" Abigail replied, and stifled a giggle.

Megan, disgusted, started to stand up to leave. If anybody had a right to gush over Jason, it was her. Not some Johnny-come-lately floozy, which was what her father called Abigail.

But Abigail grabbed her sleeve and pulled her back

down. "You don't have to go so soon, do you? I think he's about to take off his shirt."

Jason splashed water over his face, then wiped himself as dry as he could with his sweaty shirt. It was past noon, and they weren't done yet.

The water had receded nearly back to yesterday morning's levels, which gave him hope, but the men were tired and sore and out of sorts, and weren't moving as fast as they had the previous day.

Still, he held out hope that they'd finish by mid-afternoon. He wanted to get across this creek today, by God.

Wiping his brow on a bandanna, Saul Cohen came up next to him and momentarily rested his shovel against a rock. "I didn't think it was supposed to be so hot this early in the season," he said.

"It's not," said Jason. "We just got lucky."

"We're lucky with both heat and water," Saul mused. "It could be worse. There could be more snakes."

Jason said, "Yeah, I suppose there could." Just that morning, Rachael had killed a rattler hiding in their temporary woodpile.

Saul helped himself to a dipper of fresh water from the bucket. "How many more?"

Jason cocked a brow. "How many more what?"

"Branches of this river?"

"None."

Saul pursed his lips. "But other creeks, other rivers?"

"Yes."

Saul picked up his shovel. "With fords or ferries or bridges already there, one could hope. Just so it shouldn't be boring."

Jason lifted his shovel, too. "These treks rarely are, Saul. Boring is what you pray for."

"The Good Lord didn't have his ear turned toward

you on that one, Fury," broke in Mel Sanderson, one of Colorado Gooding's men. "Appears he didn't hear any of us." Sanderson picked up the dipper that Saul had just put down and helped himself to the water.

"I couldn't say, Sanderson," Jason told him. "But so far, we're alive, aren't we?"

"At least, most of us are," cut in a sweaty Matt MacDonald, who had just stepped up for his turn at the fresh water.

Jason didn't answer him. "Back to work, men," he said, and started back to the dig.

Behind him, he heard Sanderson say, "Don't believe that Jason feller likes you much, son."

And Matt MacDonald's growled reply: "The feeling's mutual."

20

By four o'clock, most of the wagons had successfully forded the creek, and were setting up a new camp about one hundred yards from the point of crossing. Jason was still busy at the ford, though, helping the remaining wagons across the stream, then climbing back up the muddy slope they had dug down to it.

Last of all came the Wheelers' iron-bottom wagon, which managed to sink into a creek bed that had held up under the previous wagons just fine. Jason had to run and borrow a couple of oxen from one of the other wagons to help pull it up.

But he got the job done, then brought the herd and remuda across. They were the easiest, although the hogs and goats were a little cranky about being asked to ford something that was deeper than they were tall.

Everybody made it fine, though.

By five, the women were cooking dinner. Mel Sanderson had produced a harmonica and proved to be pretty darned good with it. When she felt the song was godly enough, Mrs. Milcher accompanied him from inside her wagon, on the piano.

Jason leaned back against the side of his wagon, where Jenny and Megan sat on a blanket. "Three hundred yards in a day," he grumbled, shaking his head. "Pa would be plain embarrassed."

Jenny looked up. "Papa would be proud, and you know it, Jason."

"He thought seven miles a day on the flat was bad."

"That wasn't counting digging fords," she said. "How long til we get to Santa Fe?"

"A week, maybe, if we're lucky. We've got the Sangre de Cristo foothills to contend with."

Mrs. Milcher stopped playing, for Sanderson had turned to playing a lively jig and Colorado had pulled out a fiddle and was playing along, with a great deal of enthusiasm if not much talent. Several couples were dancing.

Megan stood up and shyly held her hand toward Jason just as Abigail Krimp came up from the other side and grabbed his arm. "Let's dance, Jason," Abigail said, pulling him toward her.

He didn't have much choice. He followed her out to where the other pilgrims were dancing, and joined in. When he turned back toward the wagon, Megan had disappeared.

The trail, which had become frequently used enough to show ruts, split into a Y in the foothills. And about six feet from that very spot, Hamish MacDonald and Jason were having a difference of opinion.

"I say we go up," Hamish insisted, pointing toward the right hand arm of the Y. "Right is over the mountain. We'll save time."

"It'll take us over the foothills, all right, but it's tricky. We're bound to lose some wagons, maybe people. I won't chance it, Hamish."

"You're loony, lad. Look how deep those ruts are! It looks to me as if more than half the travelers that have passed this way have taken that route!"

It was all Jason could do not to slap the old man right

across his ruddy whiskers. He said, "We're taking the low road, Hamish. Around the foothills, not through them. You can do as you damn well please. I'm sick and tired of fighting with you."

And then he just rode off, shouting to the wagons directly behind to follow him, and left Hamish sitting his horse in their path.

He didn't look back for quite some time, being content to ease along the trail followed by the clanks and rumbles of wagons and the rhythmic plods of hooves. But when he did glance up, he caught sight of something that made his stomach turn over—Hamish MacDonald's wagon, driven by Hamish himself, with Matthew up front on horseback.

It didn't make him ill that Hamish wanted to chance killing himself, and it certainly didn't bother him that Matthew was up there—but Megan . . . Had Megan followed her father and taken the mountain trail? Was she in that wagon?

Leaving Ward to lead the caravan, he galloped back to his own rig, only to find Jenny deep in conversation with Megan.

"Megan," he cried in relief. "You didn't go with your father and brother!"

Megan said, "They're crazy. I told them that if I couldn't stop them from killing themselves, I could at least save myself." Then she added, "They won't get killed, will they? I mean, not really?'

"They had a big fight over it, Jason," Jenny interjected. He didn't understand why, but Jenny acted as if she'd rather they hadn't left the rest of the train. Jenny knew what a pain in the butt Hamish had always been, and the trouble Jason continually had with Matt.

Megan said, "You've got to stop them, Jason! I know they're both bullheaded, but . . . I mean, I was only trying to . . ." And then she doubled over and began to weep.

Before Jason realized it, he had leapt from Cleo's back to the wagon seat and taken Megan into his arms. Jenny, sitting just beyond Megan, arched her brows, glanced heavenward.

"Megan, it's too late," he began.

She sobbed harder.

"Megan, I didn't mean . . . what I meant to say was that it's too late for them to turn their rig around. They'd have to back the Conestoga down that narrow trail, and that's a lot more dangerous than just going on ahead. They'll be fine up there if they're careful."

Sniffling, she lifted her face and looked into his eyes. "Really?" she asked.

Her eyes, cheeks, and nose were reddened with weeping and moist with tears, and for some reason he couldn't help thinking that she'd never looked more beautiful. He couldn't help himself. He kissed her.

Her lips were soft and warm. He heard his sister hiss, *"Jason!"*

Blinking rapidly, he pulled away. Megan's face was filled with questions, Jenny's with outright shock and surprise. He felt heat shoot up his neck and fill his cheeks.

He scooted away to the very edge of the bench, then dropped down and off the wagon. It was a miracle he landed on his feet, he was shaking so hard. The big wheels rolled on by him. Megan's head appeared briefly, peeking around the edge of the canvas roof. And then somebody jerked her back. Undoubtedly Jenny.

He whistled for Cleo, and the palomino came trotting up. He remounted, wondering why just kissing a girl would have such an effect on him! But this was no Washington-soiled dove or Kansas City whore. This was the girl he was going to marry.

Marry? Where had that come from?

* * *

"Megan MacDonald!" Jenny scolded as she jerked Megan back, momentarily incensed that her best friend had allowed Jason to kiss her in public. Especially when that same best friend had been so unpleasant about Jenny's confessed feelings for Matt.

She was still mad about it, even though she had pretended to forgive Megan. It just made things easier, that was all—it wasn't as if Jenny could just find a new best friend in the little community of the train.

But this new affront was too much!

"What do you mean by kissing my brother?" she asked. "I mean, right out here in front of God and everybody?"

Megan had a slightly dazed look on her face. She said, "I didn't kiss him. He kissed me." And then she smiled, just like a cat in the cream, and leaned back. "He kissed me!"

"You sure stopped crying quick."

Megan didn't answer.

Jenny frowned. "Maybe you'd better fill me in with the rules for this sort of thing. I'm probably too young to understand," she added sarcastically, "but I'll try."

Megan turned toward her. "Understand what?"

"Why it's all right for you to make eyes at my brother all the time, and for you to kiss him right out where anybody can see you, but it's not all right for me to do the same with *your* brother. Don't you think I'm good enough for your precious Matthew?"

Megan said, "Just the opposite, Jenny. I don't think he's good enough for *you*."

"Jason, oh, Jason!" Abigail Krimp waved her hankie at him from the driver's seat of Nordstrom's spare wagon and, reluctantly, he made his way over. She was all dolled up today—looked like she'd just walked out of a saloon, actually—in spangles and sparkly things and cheap jewelry.

"Hello, Miss Abigail," he said, and tipped his hat as he rode alongside the wagon. "What can I do for you this afternoon?"

"Oh, nothing, nothing at all, Jason," she said. She dabbed the hankie at her own neck—and chest, most of which was exposed. "I just wanted to tell you what a fine dancer you are. In case I didn't last night, I mean. Because you really are. A good dancer, I mean."

"I, uh . . . Thank you," he said, flustered. "Well, I'd best get back up front."

"Oh, don't go quite so soon," Abigail said, before he had a chance to show Cleo his heels. "Did you know that we had such talented musicians in our very midst?"

"My pa said something about Colorado playing the fiddle." Badly.

"I thought he was just grand, didn't you?"

"I really have to—"

"Jason!" Ward Wanamaker galloped toward him from the front of the train. "Jason, come quick!"

Grateful for the excuse to turn his back on Abigail Krimp, Jason pushed Cleo from a walk directly into a lope and rode up to see what was agitating Ward.

When they met, Ward looked as shook up as a bottle of over-warm sarsaparilla, ready to explode. "You've got to come up front!" he shouted.

Jason held his hands over his ears—Ward was only a couple feet from him, but he was yelling like he was still six wagons away.

"Sorry," Ward said, still excited, but less loud. "There's been an accident."

Hamish had fallen off the damned mountain. That was the first thought that came into his head.

But Ward followed up with, "It's the Milchers. They busted a wheel all to smash!"

Well, that was just wonderful, wasn't it? "I don't suppose they've got a spare?"

Ward blinked. "You know, I didn't think to ask 'em."

"Well, get up there and do it." Ward galloped off, and Jason turned his attention to slowing up and halting the other wagons. When he came to Salmon Kendall's rig, Salmon asked if he needed a hand, which Jason gratefully accepted.

Salmon untied his saddle horse from the rear of his wagon, tightened its girth, and swung up into the saddle. "If they don't got a spare, I do, and so do the MacDonalds and Saul," he said as they jogged forward. "There's probably more, but I don't—"

"The MacDonalds' spare wheel is probably halfway up the mountainside," Jason said, "but I'm glad to know that you and Saul both have one." More like, he was pleased to hear that a couple of his employers weren't complete idiots. But he didn't say so.

Instead, he said, "I thought an extra wagon wheel was on Pa's 'necessities list' for each wagon, right along with a rifle and water."

"It was, Jason, it was."

21

As it turned out, an extra wagon wheel was one of the "frills" the Reverend Milcher had thrown out so he could fit his new piano in the wagon. And Saul Cohen had the misfortune of being in the wagon right in front of the Milchers, and thus was deprived of his spare.

"Sorry, Saul," Jason said as they watched Milcher, Salmon, Colorado, and Milt Billings lever Milcher's wagon up onto a makeshift support consisting of Mrs. Milcher's marble-topped dresser. Milcher had done a job on his wheel, all right. If he had tried to find the biggest, most jagged boulder to run over, he couldn't have done a better job. Jason had Ward slapping whitewash on the offending rock, to mark it out for the following wagons.

Saul was philosophical about the whole thing, though. He shrugged and said, "It's good to help the man who hates you. He might come in handy later on. At least, that's what my Uncle Nathan used to say, and didn't he die the wealthiest Jew in New Jersey?"

Jason thumbed back his hat and said, "Guess I never thought about it that way. But you're right."

The humiliation of it was written all over Milcher's face. It must be eating him up inside to think that he and his kin were going to make it only because a heathen Hebrew had done him a favor.

With a loud thud, accompanied by numerous groans

and the discordant hum of piano wires, the wagon was dropped on its support. Jason said, "I sure wish that Seth Wheeler was still with us. At least he knew something about being a wheelwright."

"I haven't had a chance to see Mary since the attack," Saul said. "How is she holding up?"

"Fine, I suppose," Jason replied. "Well, as good as anybody else under the circumstances. She was a big help to Dr. Morelli. She was a nurse during the War, you know."

Saul nodded. "And, I'm told, a dance hall girl before that."

This was news to Jason. "Where'd you hear that?"

"Rachael. These women, they gossip," Saul said, staring straight ahead. "Well, they gossip and my Rachael, she keeps her ears open. Anything you want to know about the private affairs of anyone we have lived near or known or *almost* known in the past nine years, you bring yourself to Saul Cohen and ask. I'll ask Rachael for you."

The men had Milcher's old wheel pulled off. Well, it wasn't really a wheel anymore. It was just splintered wood and a bent, broken, rusty rim, which they tossed to the side in pieces.

The land they were currently stalled on had taken what Jason's father would have called "a turn for the worse." Trees, when there were any, had gone shrubby or stunted and twisted. The color of the earth varied, but was mostly the color of powdery, dried blood, and the farmers in the group had been remarking on it since they passed through Indian Territory.

Snakes were more common, as were spiders. A week earlier, Jason had called everyone around him and explained the importance of watching where they walked, a lecture that was brought on by Europa Morton, sister to their schoolmarm, having been struck by a rattler.

Usually, she was driving, for her husband, Milton, had been injured and later died during the Comanche raid, but for some reason she was on foot. She had explained that she'd heard somebody's teakettle hissing and had gone to investigate. And of course, the "hissing" she'd heard was a warning rattle from a rather old and large diamondback.

The snake was so old, in fact, that it hadn't injected enough venom to hurt anything more than her pride, but after Ezekial killed it, Jason had stretched and tanned its skin. He thought Europa might like to have it to display. Or that her father might like it for a hatband.

It turned out that neither one of them wanted the thing, but Salmon Kendall had expressed his admiration for it, so the hatband went to him. It looked a little funny on that floppy-brimmed hat he always wore, but he didn't seem to mind.

They got the new wheel in place and levered the wagon back down, although Jason thought that the "sawhorse"—Mrs. Milcher's bureau—was forever going to be the worse for wear. And they started moving again. By this time, it was nearly five, and Jason figured they could travel for perhaps another hour before they stopped for the night.

Which they did, at a wide spot on the trail that Jason had remembered. Other wagon trains had used it, too, for there were a couple of graves, marked by crude crosses, near the edge of the place, and someone had left behind an old rocking chair. Saul's eye landed on it right away, and after giving it a kick to ward off snakes, he scooped it up, vowing to repair it later.

There was still no sign of the errant MacDonalds, but Jason didn't expect it. Either they'd meet up later, in Santa Fe, or Hamish would get himself killed, regardless of anything Jason had said to Megan.

He felt oddly embarrassed by that kiss. If he'd been

thinking, if he'd been in his right mind or she hadn't looked so vulnerable, he would have restrained himself—both from the action itself, and the self-recriminations that followed. But he hadn't been and she had, and he didn't.

And it was done.

Dinner that night was a hodgepodge of game and tame animals, canned vegetables—and beans, beans, and more beans. Everybody would be glad when they got to Santa Fe and could restock their mobile pantries. Once again, the harmonica and fiddle came out for some music, or at least, something vaguely akin to music, but the piano was silent, Mrs. Milcher having said she wasn't up to playing.

Jason figured that was probably the truth. She was still embarrassed about her husband having abandoned their spare wheel in favor of the piano, and likely didn't want to be reminded so soon.

As for Jason himself, he was keeping to the shadows, huddled in conversation with Saul or Salmon on the opposite side of the circled wagons from his own wagon and Megan MacDonald. He hadn't spoken to her since making that grave error earlier in the day. At least, that was how he thought of their kiss now: his grave error.

They could have absolutely no future together. Hers lay with her father and brother, in California. His lay on the opposite side of the country. She should marry some other erstwhile pioneer. Not him.

No, not him.

Still, he couldn't help feeling drawn to her like iron filings to a magnet. How could he feel she was so right—that she was the *one*—when she was so obviously wrong for him?

His head was in danger of losing out to his heart, and

he knew it. What he didn't know was that, being young, he was unintentionally callous, and this was why he avoided her now.

"What?" he muttered, vaguely aware that Saul had said something.

Saul looked confused. "Nothing. I just asked if you need more coffee."

Jason shook his head. "No, thanks."

"We keep eating beans like this, and Rachael, for once, will be glad to be sleeping in an open wagon."

Jason smiled a little.

"It's a girl, isn't it?" Saul asked. "The reason you're acting so strangely, that is. For a minute, I thought maybe you were mad at me for volunteering my spare wheel. But now I'm thinking that maybe you've got woman trouble. Why else would you hide over here, with a couple of old married people?"

It took Jason a moment to realize that the "old married people" Saul referred to were himself and Rachael.

"Don't be silly," Jason said. "Unless you want to get rid of me?" He started to stand up, thinking he'd overstayed his welcome.

But Saul put a hand on his arm. "No, no. Sit and make yourself comfortable. And tell me—who is she, this girl who has you tied in such knots? Is it the lovely Miss Krimp?"

Jason snorted.

"I take it this is a *no*?"

"You take it right."

"Ah. Megan MacDonald, then."

Jason turned toward him.

"Didn't I know it? Rachael," he called. "We were right."

Jason snapped, "Keep your voice down!" before he realized his mouth was moving. And then he muttered, "Sorry, Saul."

"No apology is needed. I remember what it was like

with my Rachael, and I wasn't trying to keep twenty-some wagons safe on the way west. You have quite a lot to handle, Jason."

More than Saul knew, Jason thought. "I can't. Not right now."

"You can't fall in love *now?*" Saul's eyebrows went up. "Love isn't something you can give yourself permission for. You can't pick the time and place, or the girl. Love is God's gift to you and a woman, forever and always."

"Well, He sure picked a bad time to give it to me."

Saul threw his arms into the air. "The young," he said, shaking his head. "So ungrateful."

"Jason?" Jenny's voice.

"Over here, Jenny."

She came from the next wagon in line, her skirts held up in clenched fists and swishing angrily before her, and Jason thought, *I'm in for it now!*

"Jason Fury!" she began. "Have you been over here all the evening? I've been looking for you. *Megan's* been looking for you!" Just then, she saw Saul and said, "Good evening, Mr. Cohen."

Saul nodded and said, "Good evening, Jenny," adding, "Please, don't let me stop your conversation. I'm not here." He leaned back against the wheel spokes and straightened his legs out before him.

Jason barely heard him. He said, "Megan?"

"Well, no, not actually," Jenny admitted angrily. "But if I were her, I would have dogged you all over camp!"

"You did," Jason said.

"Oh. Well . . . can we go somewhere and talk?" Her eyes slid toward Saul, then back to Jason again.

But Jason had no intention of going anywhere. "No. Just tell her . . . just tell her I'm sorry if I embarrassed her."

"Embarrassed her!"

Clearly, if Jenny got any more steamed up, she'd whistle like a teakettle.

"Jen, it's none of your business!" he said. "Now, go back to the wagon."

"None of my business? It's none of my business when my own brother—?"

"I said, go back to the wagon," he snapped, cutting her off. "Now, Jenny. I mean it."

She must have taken his glower seriously, because she stood there a moment, her mouth hanging open, then turned away. But she stopped walking for a second, just long enough to turn back and hiss, "Coward!" at him.

Jason stood there, watching her march back across the circle, before he gratefully slid back down and landed beside Saul.

"Sorry," he said.

"Women," Saul said.

"Exactly. Women."

Saul paused for a few moments before he said, "Whatever it is, you'd better fix it tonight. Be a *mensch*."

Jason still hadn't looked at him. "Yeah. I guess so." Jenny'd been right. He was a coward. All she'd done was point it out.

Damn it. Belatedly, he looked over at Saul and raised a brow. "A *mensch*?"

"Be a man, Jason. A human being."

22

Be a mensch, he told himself as he rose and walked, like he was heading for the gallows, to his wagon. Megan was nowhere in sight, but he couldn't think where else she would be staying other than with Jenny, what with her pa and brother having taken the upper trail.

Hell, half the time she spent the night with Jenny, anyway. Jason had been sleeping under Salmon Kendall's wagon.

He reached the Conestoga and stood there for a moment, wondering what to do next—other than turn tail and hoof it back to the East Coast, which was his first thought.

"Welcome home." Jenny's voice. He turned toward it. She hung out of the back of the wagon, off the tailgate, and her face was as stern as her voice. For a moment, she wasn't his little sister at all. She was his mother.

"You were right," he said, attempting to keep his voice flat and even. He sure didn't feel that way. "Where's Megan?"

Saul shook his head as he watched their young leader. "I wouldn't wish to be in his boots tonight for all the cream cheese in . . . where do they make cream cheese, Rachael?"

"Where they have many milk cows. Saul, don't you think you're taking too much on yourself?"

"Because I am curious about cream cheese?" He shrugged. "I would like some right now. From New York City, where there are no Indians."

She felt his forehead. "Why are you talking crazy, all of a sudden?"

He reached up, took her hand, and held it in both of his. "Is it so crazy to wonder about a boy wooing a girl when it's possible that he's let her family stray into the hands of the heathen horde?"

Rachael rolled her eyes and withdrew her hand. "You're talking of the MacDonalds?"

"Who else?"

Rachael pulled over her little milking stool and sat down on it. "And the Comanche?"

Saul nodded.

"We haven't seen them for weeks," she said. "Why should we see them now?"

"Perhaps we are too many. Perhaps young Quanah Parker spares us, for some reason known only to himself and God. Who's to know? But out there, one wagon, alone?"

"You shouldn't even mention it, Saul," Rachael said with a shudder.

"Why not? You think, from my lips to God's ears?"

"You don't think it's bad luck to joke about such things?"

He took her hand again and patted it. "All right, Rachael. Don't be worrying your head."

There was a long silence, during which they sat there, him holding her hand. And then, at last, she said, "Saul?"

"What, my love?"

"Saul, I am in a family way again."

He looked up at her, looked up at this beautiful woman whom God had chosen for him, the woman who had left all she knew to come west with him. How had he ever deserved her?

He put his hand on her belly. It was still very flat. At least, by what he could feel through all the layers of clothing that women wore. "How soon?"

"Seven months, perhaps seven and a half. We will be settled in our new home by then. I am hoping for a girl this time. A girl is all right?"

Megan couldn't believe what she was hearing. It didn't make any sense. It was all she could do not to burst into tears, but she hung on, hung on because it seemed to confuse him so much when she cried. At least, that was what he was blaming for kissing her this afternoon.

Blame?

How could such a wonderful thing, such a perfect and sublime thing, need somewhere to lay blame?

"Do you understand, Megan?" he asked. He hadn't touched her, not with the tiniest tip of his finger. He'd purposely stayed at the opposite end of the wagon from her. There was only one lamp lit, and she could barely make any of him out except for a glimmer of his profile. It danced with his every movement.

"No, I don't understand, Jason. Explain again how your kissing me affects some college back East?"

Once again, he bumbled into a long, convoluted explanation that made no sense whatsoever. But she understood that she was listening to a young man desperately trying to talk himself out of loving her. Without much success, it seemed.

She clasped her hands in her lap and said, "You love me, Jason. And I love you, too."

* * *

Far away on the upper trail, Hamish MacDonald poured himself another cup of coffee. "And Megan said we couldn't feed ourselves without her!"

Sitting across the small fire, Matt lit a cigarette. He hadn't been much for smoking before, but ever since he'd learned that Nordstrom's extra wagon carried an ample supply of ready-mades, he'd gone to town on them. He threw the twig he'd used to light it back into the fire, and said, "She was just about right, too."

His father said, "I'll grant you, I've had better jackrabbit on this journey—"

"Didn't help that it fell in the fire," Matt cut in.

"—but not all that much superior."

"Also didn't help that you didn't notice it for a good fifteen minutes."

His father shot him a glance that fairly blistered, and Matt quickly added, "Or me, either."

Hamish's scowl evaporated. "That's right, by God. You didn't notice it, either, laddie."

"No, Pa." His father had been touchy all day. No use in baiting him now.

"That's more like it," Hamish said in a grumble, and pulled out a cigar.

"When you think we'll make Santa Fe?" Matt asked.

Hamish searched the edge of the fire for a twig, then gave up and pulled out a match. "Your guess is as good as mine."

Hamish puffed at the cigar, lighting it. Why did he have to smoke that smelly tobacco? Lord knows, he could afford better. Judging from the fumes, it had to taste awful, like a mouthful of pig swill, Matt imagined. But if it was the cheapest possible but looked good, his pa would buy it.

That was how his pa did everything—shit on the inside, gold foil on the outside.

Except for those Morgan mares of his. They were bred to the nines, each and every one. Matt had nearly wet himself when he learned what his father had paid for just one mare. Funny, him leaving them behind with the herd and the main wagon train when he was so sure he had found a superior route.

Superior route? Hell, Hamish and that damned wagon had nearly fallen down the mountain at least three times today. Once, Matt had to hitch his saddle horse to the front end of the team to help get the Conestoga back up on the trail. It was the last thing that Matt wanted to admit, but he wished his father had listened to Jason Fury this time.

The trail was terrible—narrow and rocky and rutted—and they had several times seen the traces of scraped earth left by some long-ago, ill-fated wagon that had tumbled over the edge, dislodging rock as it went. If it weren't for his father's wishes—and the fact that he knew it would tick Jason Fury off—he'd be down below, taking the easier trail with the rest of the party. And to tell the truth, he had come more to irritate Jason than to please his father.

Too bad that Jenny had to be a Fury, Matt thought. She was a little young, but she was sure a looker. If you liked the wholesome type, which Matt usually didn't.

But he figured he could make an exception for Jenny Fury.

Sooner or later, that stuck-up, pigheaded brother of hers would head back East to go to some fancy college, and Matt figured that by the time that happened, Jenny would be more than willing to stay behind. With him, and as a MacDonald.

"What are you thinking about?" came his father's rumbling voice. "You look like the cat who swallowed the canary bird."

"Nothing," Matt said, embarrassed to have been betrayed by his own expression. "Just thinkin', that's all."

"Well, don't look so damned smug."

Matt exhaled his last lungful of smoke through his nose in two jets of yellowish air. Smug, indeed! He *ought* to be smug. Pretty soon he'd be in California, set with a wife, rid of Jason Fury, and first in line to inherit enough good cattle and horses to make him a big man, no matter where they settled.

That is, if his father didn't get them both killed on this mountain trail.

23

Olympia Morelli saw it first, and screamed. Dr. Morelli, driving the wagon, saw where she was looking and immediately hauled back hard on the team's reins, crying, "Look out, look out!"

Having managed to halt his wagon in time, Morelli leapt down to see to Olympia. She was mere days away from giving birth, and had only just climbed down from the wagon to stretch her legs. Now she stood about twenty feet away from the wagon, hands over her mouth, and she would not stop screaming.

Other women took up the cry as Conestogas hastily pulled out of line to avoid the hail of wagon parts and tumbling livestock and broken furniture and stray rock that came down the mountainside like so much confetti, thrown by a careless giant.

When it was all done, Hamish MacDonald was in their midst again, although only his scraped and twisted corpse. He rolled and bumped to a halt against the off-lead horse of Salmon Kendall's wagon, spooking the animal so badly that Salmon nearly lost his rig, too.

Dodging flying chunks of wagon, Morelli left his wife and ran to the body, but there was nothing that could be done. Hamish's face was pulp—raw flesh, decorated here and there by cactus thorns—and he no longer breathed.

For not the first time in his career, Morelli saw death

as a blessing. He could tell with a quick glance that aside from the surface damage, Hamish had sustained two broken arms—both compound fractures—and a leg broken so badly that it was twisted like a licorice stick.

Morelli didn't have time to look very long, though. Salmon Kendall grabbed him by the arm and yanked an instant before part of a wheel landed on the corpse, followed by a broken axle.

"Thank you, Salmon," he yelled. All that debris coming down the mountainside made a deadly rumble and racket.

Salmon nodded at him, then pulled him farther toward the back of the wagon, around it, and then off the trail. Olympia was still there, although she wasn't standing any longer. She was on the ground. He ran toward her.

"I'm sorry, Michael," she said when he got there. "My water broke."

As the last of the debris thudded and skittered down upon them, he helped her to her feet and to their wagon, where their children waited, huddled and afraid.

"Pa!" Matt called down the mountainside.

No answer, except for the retreating noise of torn rock and a wagon turned into toothpicks. Everything that was his and Megan's in this world, including their father.

To him, the wagon had simply disappeared after its outside wheels slipped off the trail. The Conestoga skidded and tumbled, turning twice over and spewing its contents like a burst canning jar before it went over the abrupt edge of a cliff.

From then on out, he only heard its progress.

Roughly, he wiped at his face, but he was still shaking

from the shock, his burning eyes still brimming from the loss. He swung down off his horse, but his legs didn't hold him up. He sat down on the trail, just where his boots landed, and he began to sob.

This is that damn Jason Fury's fault!

Below, the wagons had finally pulled clear of the section of trail where the remains of Hamish MacDonald's wagon rested. A grave had been quickly, if not easily, dug, and Hamish himself had been buried and spoken over, and the grave marked by a crude cross.

His dead and battered draft animals had been covered over with kerosene and brush and set alight, and a weeping Megan—aided by Jenny and a few of the women—had picked up the precious few items not ruined and stowed them in the Furys' wagon.

But Hamish's belongings weren't the only ones to suffer. Carrie English's wagon had been plowed into by the front half of Hamish's Conestoga, crushing her front wheel, and again they had a wheel to change. Fortunately, she was carrying a spare.

One of Hamish's dead horses had slammed into the Milchers' team and broken the leg of the off-wheel horse, necessitating its being shot. Assorted wagon debris had landed on Randall Nordstrom's second wagon and broken two of the wooden hoops that held the canvas up. Nordstrom had tried to figure how to fix them for the longest time, then given up and just strapped the canvas down, over the load.

And Jason kicked himself. Why had he dared Hamish to go up there in the first place? He should have just knocked him out and thrown him in his own wagon, then let Megan drive it. By the time Hamish came around again, they would have been well enough along that he wouldn't have turned back.

Everybody would be safe and sound.

And they wouldn't be stopped again, here in this clearing, trying to put themselves back together while Hamish's horses sent up pillars of blackish smoke in the distance, and Mr. Morelli delivered his wife, and the Widow English nursed a broken arm.

And where the heck was Matt MacDonald? Not that Jason really cared. He supposed Matt was still up there, someplace. Alone.

And for a moment, he *did* care about Matt. He knew what it was like to lose your father. He wouldn't want to be alone at such a time as this.

"Jason?"

He turned his head. "Yes, Jenny?"

She looked overly tired and washed out. "The Morellis. They've had a little boy. His name is Rubio. Mrs. Wheeler helped midwife."

"Congratulations to the Morellis, then," he replied, although he lacked enthusiasm. Somehow, he couldn't drum up much for a new life when so many people were leaving this world in such a hurry. Hell, if he hadn't known better, he would have thought there was a going-out-of-business sale up in heaven.

"How's Megan doing?" he asked.

"She'll be all right," Jenny replied. "She usually is, though I don't know about a time like this."

"Jenny, I've been thinking. Papa had a good friend in Santa Fe, Wash Keough. Been thinking that maybe I ought to leave you there till I can come back for you."

Her head snapped up again. "What?"

"I said, I've been thinking that—"

She pushed away his arm. "Oh, I heard you, Jason Fury. You will not drop me off along the trail, you hear me?"

"But I thought you might be happier if—"

"Since when is anybody concerned about *my* happiness? I won't stay, I tell you. I'll grab the first horse I see and take out after you."

He slid his arm around her stiff little shoulders. "Now, now, Jen. Can't have you hanged for a horse thief. Guess I'll have to take you all the way with me, then, just to keep you out of prison."

Some of the stiffness went out of her, and she said, "You promise? You know, they hang horse thieves."

He nodded. "I know. And I promise, Jenny, you won't hang."

Night fell.

Matt MacDonald crouched in front of his fire, alone, missing his father's company.

No, not really. Not missing his company. Just . . . regretful. And put out.

Yes, put out. It was all so damned inconvenient. Well, he did feel a little sad about his father, but was it only because he was supposed to? Was it just because he was used to him? After all, Hamish was the only father he'd ever known. He was the only grown man he'd known all his life. He supposed he should feel sorrow.

But mostly, he felt put upon for having to ride up this damned mountain in the first place, and for having to watch all his belongings tumble down all to Hell. Also, for the knowledge that he was going to have to navigate this lousy excuse for a trail all the way to Santa Fe, and all by himself.

And for the fact that he had no dinner. He hadn't seen hide nor hair of a bird, let along a jackrabbit, all damn afternoon. All he had along was some hardtack, in bits in the bottom of his saddlebags, and he'd eaten the last crumbs by about four o'clock. He was thinking very fondly of beans and beef. He'd just have to do without. Tomorrow he could find something to shoot and eat.

He wondered if the train had come across what remained of his father and the rig. He wondered if it had even rolled and fallen that far, or if it had crashed behind them. Nothing could have survived that fall. Not a horse, not his father. Not the wagon. Nothing.

Stomach growling, he lay down in the middle of that rutted trail and tried to sleep.

24

Several days later, when Jason and the wagons pulled into the dusty town of Santa Fe, Matt was waiting for them. He waited until he saw Jason dismount. Then he walked out into the open, right up to him, tapped him on the shoulder, and slugged him in the jaw when he turned around.

Having rehearsed this scene in his mind over and over, he had expected Jason to go down. Maybe even fly back a couple of feet.

But not only did he not go down, he punched back. Hard. The blow to his stomach sent Matt back, doubled over and staggering and waiting for Jason to strike again, but he didn't. He just stood there, glowering and rubbing his face.

"What's your problem, MacDonald?" he half-shouted.

Men from the other wagons were running up by this time. Through the pain, Matt heard Saul Cohen shouting something or other. He hoped it was, "Jason's gone crazy! Get him!"

But apparently, it wasn't, because when Saul's boot steps reached Matt, he felt arms wrestle him to the ground, and finally realized that Saul Cohen and Salmon Kendall had him down and pinned. "You idiot," Saul hissed into his ear.

"Let go!" he shouted. "I'm gonna kill you, Jason Fury!"

He heard, more than felt, somebody slip the revolvers from his holsters, and then arms yanked him to his feet.

"Señores," came an unfamiliar voice, "is there a problem?"

The voice belonged to a big Mexican, complete with badge. "Must I repeat myself?" he asked, and this time he looked a little perturbed.

"There's no problem," said Jason, as Kendall and Cohen slowly released Matthew. Matt shook himself out.

"No," Matt said, glaring at Jason. "No problem at all." *That you need to butt into.*

The deputy stood there a moment longer, until he was satisfied there wasn't going to be a fistfight, Matt supposed, and then he walked on without further word. When he passed out of sight, Kendall and Cohen released Matt, although they both stood too close. Matt took a step forward, toward Jason.

"My pa's dead because of you," he said. "That's something I won't forget. Ever. You get me?"

Jason said, "Don't suppose you will. Even if it's not true."

Saul Cohen butted in. "Now, Matthew, your papa made his own decision. Didn't we all hear him, Salmon?"

"I sure did," Salmon Kendall agreed. "Heard him plain."

"Just be thankful you were with him," Saul added. "He might not have lasted so long as he did without his blood beside him."

Jason remained silent.

Matt pretended he hadn't heard a word out of either Saul or Salmon and grumbled, "You'll pay for this, Fury. Sooner or later, you'll pay and I'll be there, takin' the toll."

* * *

After getting the last wagon in place and seeing that each family was settled in, Jason set out to see the dusty little town of Santa Fe and look up his father's old friend, Wash Keough. Saul tagged along, with a shopping list from Rachael tucked into his pocket.

Santa Fe was a wonderland to Saul. Most of the buildings were made of a clay mud—which, Jason informed him, was called adobe—which was whitewashed to glimmer in the sun. Some buildings were plainly Spanish in their architecture, and others were, well, American. Plain. A little dirty-looking.

Saul was shocked at the dead animals left to rot in the streets, though Jason seemed to pay them no mind. He was aghast when they passed a cantina that looked to be a brothel, too, and when he stopped to watch a wheelwright at work, crafting spindles for a buggy wheel, Jason had to tug on his arm to get him moving again.

"This is some strange place," he said. They passed a beautiful señorita, dressed all in black and followed by an older woman and two men carrying guns.

Jason saw him looking and said, "That's Miss Constanza Corboda, with her companion and her bodyguards. Rich, really Old World Spanish, if you know what I mean."

Saul didn't, but nodded his head anyway. He was too busy taking everything in to be distracted by explanations.

At last, Jason turned into the front walk of a small white house, adobe in construction, and rapped on the turquoise-painted, chipped front door. Red, dried, and hard fruits of some kind hung on it in a huge bunch.

"That's called a *chile ristra*," said Jason.

The door opened and a smallish, gray-haired man with his hair in a long horse tail—nearly to his waist—a

face like an ax blade, a big grizzled mustache, and a little potbelly under his long pink underwear stood there
for a moment, then cried out, "Jason? Jason Fury?" and
latched onto the boy like a starving tick to a passing
dog. Saul noted that the horse tail was so long that the
very ends of it were still shot through with a little brown.

Jason slapped the old fellow on his back, crying,
"Howdy, Wash. How goes it?"

"Fine, fine," said the man, who Saul guessed to be
Wash Keough. "Well, come in! What you doin', standin'
on a man's front stoop all the day?"

Saul followed Jason in, although he had yet to be introduced. However, Mr. Keough didn't seem too inclined toward the formalities, so Saul decided he needn't
be, either. He waited until Keough led them to the kitchen
and put on the coffeepot before he stuck out his hand
and said, "Saul Cohen, sir. It's an honor to make your
acquaintance."

"Well, I'm sorry there, Mr. Cohen," Keough boomed
happily. He was short, but he filled the room, and Saul
could see why he had been a friend of Jedediah Fury.
Both of them were larger-than-life characters. "I'm
right pleased to meet you," he went on, still pumping
Saul's hand. "Any friend of Jason's is a friend'a mine.
Where's your pa, anyhow, Jason? That ol' mule skinner
owes me a game'a checkers."

He let go of Saul's hand, and Saul fairly collapsed
into a chair. He tried not to listen while Jason told
Keough about his father's death. The words of it
washed over him, but he heard the thickness in Jason's
voice, and the sorrow in the voices of both men.

He fervently hoped that no one would cry, and then
said a quick prayer for forgiveness. He shouldn't be
worried about being embarrassed at a time like this.

But no one cried, thank God. In fact, no one so

much as spoke a word once the news had been passed on. Keough poured out the coffee, or at least, what was passing for it, then joined them at the crude table.

"That's tough," Keough said at last. "That's mighty tough for you, Jason. But it had to happen sooner or later. A man pushes his luck with redskins too much, he's bound to get arrow-shot sooner or later. You're damn lucky they didn't take off with all your women-folk, too."

Jason sighed, and then launched into the story of trailing Quanah Parker, and the subsequent dice game for the girls and the livestock.

Despite his sorrow over Jedediah's death, Wash Keough seemed to find this part hilarious. He laughed and laughed, and Saul found himself wondering if the man would think it so amusing if he had been there.

"Jason, you say Saul here thought up makin' the dice?" he boomed.

Saul nodded weakly, just remembering how scared he'd been. How scared they'd *all* been.

Suddenly, Keough slapped him on the back. "By God, Saul, that was some kind of quick thinking! Jedediah would'a been proud of the both'a you! So, where you headed this time, Jason? California? Arizona? Maybe up Denver way?"

As it turned out, it didn't much matter to Wash Keough where their destination was. He was passing fifty, had not one cent to his name, and he was ready for a new start. Jason figured it was about the fifteenth new start Wash had undertaken.

Jason was happy for him to tag along. Hell, he was delighted to hire him and pay him thirty dollars and found. Wash was as close a thing to a mountain man as they were likely to run across, and he'd traversed the trail west more than most. Probably about as many times as Jedediah had, if not more.

But there was one thing—Wash had to "test out the grub" before he made his final decision.

"Be proud for you to," Jason said as they all three walked back through town, to the place where Jason had left the wagons. "We've got a mess of really good cooks. You'll be surprised."

"Hope so, Jason," Wash said.

"*Oy!*" Saul said suddenly. He stopped and put a hand over his heart. "Rachael's list!"

"Better take care of that, Saul," Jason said with a smile. "She'll have your guts for garters otherwise."

Saul wiggled his brows. "I assure you, Mr. Keough, the ramifications would not be so terrible." He plucked the list from his pocket. "But almost." Saul ducked into the nearest mercantile.

"Hope he don't forget sugar cubes," said Wash, trying to appear philosophical, "in case we run into some like-minded Apaches."

"Good thinking," said Jason.

They had walked to the southernmost part of town, where the wagons waited, before either of them spoke again.

"Got a sizable herd there, boy," Wash commented.

"It's smaller when everybody's hitched up," Jason said, before he thought.

"Well, of course it is," Wash snapped. "You take me for an idiot?" Then his mood lightened considerably. "Say, what's that I smell? Is that fried taters and onions?" He sniffed the air again. "Is that beef? I ain't had beef in a coon's age, let alone woman-cookin'!"

Jason said, "You'll have both tonight, Wash. While we're waiting, let me introduce you around."

"Just don't go 'specting me to recamember half the folks I shake hands with. Never was good with names, and I find I'm gettin' worse in my old age."

Jason introduced him to nearly everyone in the caravan, and spent the time walking between wagons to give him a quick rundown on everyone he'd just met.

"That's gal's mighty sweet on you," Wash said after they left Abigail Krimp's wagon.

"The feeling's not mutual."

"You got somebody else?"

"No. Yes . . . I mean, no."

Olympia Morelli, the newborn strapped to her back like an Indian papoose, was up and around and directing the meal preparation. Rachael Cohen shot Jason a questioning glance when the introductions were made, and Jason quickly said, "Saul's at the mercantile."

"So where else should he be?" she replied with a shrug.

"Them wouldn't happen to be dried apple pies bakin' in them covered skillets, would it?" Wash asked. His nose was working again, and he wiped away a little drool at the corner of his mustache.

"Yes, they would, Mr. Keough," Rachael answered. "I shall be sure to save you a large piece."

Jason had never seen the old desert rat beam so wide.

"What happened, Wash?" he asked. "Why are you so broke?" It appeared as if Wash hadn't eaten a decent meal in a month of Sundays with a couple of Saturdays tossed in.

"Thieves," was what Wash said. "Thieves and miscreants." He said it with a "that's that" air, and Jason didn't press him further.

Later, Wash ate with Jason, Saul, and Salmon, and Wash told Jason that he'd been eating nothing but snake for the last two weeks.

"Hell, I murdered the last jackrabbit in Santa Fe months ago," Wash said. "And I was about to run outta snake."

"Run out?" Salmon asked.

"How could a man run out of snakes in this country?" Saul asked.

Wash drew his gun and opened the chamber. "Only two slugs left, see?"

Jason said, "Don't worry. I'll supply the ammo."

"Fair 'nough." All of a sudden, he sat straight up. "That your woman I see comin' there, Saul? The one with that good apple pie all plated up?"

Again, he licked away a touch of drool at the corner of his mustache.

25

The wagon train stayed over in Santa Fe for the next day, too. Jason figured that folks needed some time to get their land legs again, and the women were especially glad for the chance to stock up for the remainder of the journey. The men took care of all sorts of little repairs that they'd let pile up, and then collected in the nearest cantinas for beer and gossip.

The women weren't the only ones who liked to talk.

Matt MacDonald wisely kept his distance. Jason didn't see him, although he heard that the few surviving possessions that were Matt's or his father's were being carried by Nordstrom, and those of his sister were being carried by, well, *him.*

Jenny at work again.

But he overheard snatches of whispers when people thought he couldn't hear. They told him nothing new, just reinforced what he already knew.

That Matthew MacDonald was planning on killing him.

There wasn't much he could do about it, save for walking up to Matt, bold-faced, and shooting him through the heart. All he could do was just wait and see what happened, try to keep an eye on the slippery son of a bitch in the meantime, and above all, stay alive.

By the time the wagons were ready to pull out and head west once more, Wash Keough had regaled the

entire camp with stories about Jedediah, running back
to when he was a trapper and ranged the Rocky Mountains. Jason noticed that the entire camp also knew
about Quanah Parker and the sugar-cube dice game
now, too.

Actually, Jason was growing a little embarrassed
about it.

He caught sight of Matt about a half hour after they
pulled out. Matt was on horseback, riding alongside the
Milchers' wagon and deep in conversation with the
Reverend Milcher. Jason preferred to think that the reverend was counseling Matt on the loss of his father, but
he couldn't help but wonder if Milcher was in on the
plan to do him harm.

But that was just stupid, wasn't it? There wouldn't be
a plan, not an organized one if he knew Matt, and even
if there was, Milcher wouldn't be in on it. He was too
much the pacifist. He could barely kill an animal for the
supper table.

Still, just the fact that Matt and Milcher were talking
made Jason a little bit mad.

And the fact that Megan was still there, constantly in
his thoughts, frustrated him no end. He had made a
point of steering clear of her.

But now they were moving again. Now they'd swing
southwest, traveling down through Chiricahua Apache
territory, and then up to Tucson. Then it would be
north a few more days until they came to the north end
of the Santa Rita range, then west over to California.

It all sounded so simple when you just thought about
the route or saw it on paper. Deceptively simple.

There were the White Mountain Apaches to get by,
then the Chiricahuas down around Apache Pass.
Apaches left and right, as thick as proverbial thieves.
The Maricopa and Hopi Indians he wasn't too worried
about, nor the Pimas, seeing as how they were fairly

peaceable by nature. But the Yaqui tribe, over by the California border country, he was very much concerned about.

And Wash was no help. Oh, he was full of stories about white men being burned or flayed or skinned alive by Apache; men having their privates hacked off—women, too—babies impaled on spears, and torture beyond any measure of reason. Jason had to warn him not to tell those tales around the other parties in the train, particularly the women.

"Aw, goldurn it, anyhow, Jason. Why you gotta take the fun outta everything?" Wash had complained. He grinned when he said it, though.

Conversely, Wash had himself been filled in on every action, idea, overstepped boundary, and implied insult suffered by each and every member of the train since they'd left Kansas City.

Now, he liked Jason and had admired his father a good deal, and he had a hard time believing that Jason had sent Matt's daddy up that hill just to fall off it. Or that if Jason had taken the southern route over the little patch of Indian Territory, they wouldn't have run into Quanah Parker and his murdering thugs. Or any number of other things that Matt MacDonald told him.

The Reverend Milcher seemed to be a troublemaker, too. Bad-mouthing Jason every chance he had, that one, then invoking the name of the Lord, like that would make everything all right. And talking bad about those folks of the Hebrew persuasion. His woman was a bit of a snob, too. She seemed offended by Wash's manner of dress. Also, his talk and his hair and, well, everything about him.

He scratched at his neck. Well, there was no pleasing some women. Maybe she thought he was Hebrew, too.

Hell, all he knew about Hebrews was that the Bible talked about them a lot, and that Jesus was one. You'd think that would be a good thing to a Bible-thumper like Milcher.

They were about four days out of Santa Fe, and Jason had put him up front, as the scout. This was fine by him. He was up here all alone, with no women to pick at him or scold him for not taking baths. Nothing but the very faint rumble of wagons behind him, nothing but the warm air and skittering critters and soaring birds before him.

It was good to get away from civilization again. To escape the hodgepodge that was Santa Fe, with its fancy Spanish self-proclaimed aristocrats and its riffraff. And everything in between. He had liked it at first, but the town had grown old on him.

He thought of himself as a man of the wild places and a man of action, not some loiterer on the fringes of civilization. He had got to feel more and more like a camp dog.

So now here he was, on the ramble once again, and with cash in his pockets, thanks to Jason Fury. He felt like a new man.

He'd been jogging along, thinking and whistling, then thinking some more for about four hours, when he saw the dust up ahead. It was a good ways off, but it was in a line, the kind that a bunch of galloping riders might make. He stared at it a couple of seconds longer, then wheeled his horse and went back to the wagons.

Better safe than sorry.

Jason gave the command to circle the wagons in tight. He figured that what Wash had seen might be Apache, but then again, it might have been a herd of wild horses or cattle, or a line of troopers. But one out of four chances was reason enough to be prepared, no matter how inconvenient for certain members of the wagon train.

Milcher, for one. He had broken a buckle on his harness, and complained about having to untie the ends.

"You should have taken care of that back in Santa Fe," Jason said.

"I couldn't," Milcher stated, in between working at the leather straps with his fingers and teeth. "It was Sunday."

This time, the circle was formed in no time, complete with the livestock in the middle, and the men also pulled the wagons snugly head-to-butt, once the teams were unhitched. Men armed themselves, women took their positions, and children and pets were tucked away in safe hiding places.

And they waited.

After what seemed a long while to Jason, the line of rising dust came into sight. It moved north of them, paralleled them for a bit, then turned north and disappeared.

"Is that all?" Saul finally asked. "Are they gone? Are we free to move again?"

Jason scratched the back of his head. He wanted to say that he was damned if he knew, but instead, he turned toward Wash. "What do you think, Wash? They go on past, or is it a trick?"

"I think I'd wait a mite if I was you, Jason. They's tricky."

"Who's tricky?" called Milcher, who had just picked up part of his buckle-less harness again. "Comanche again?"

"More like Apache," said Wash. "Course, in this country, could be either kind'a redskin."

"Either kind?" Milcher's face, already lower than a well-digger's boot, fell even further.

Salmon Kendall had walked up. "What's the deal, Jason?"

Jason straightened his hat. "Looks like we're going to wait here a little longer, Salmon. You know, to make certain they haven't circled around."

"You know best," Salmon said, and headed back to his wagon.

"Wish I did," Jason muttered as he started toward the horizon where the dust cloud had disappeared. "I wish to hell that I did."

Two hours later, there was still no sign of marauding heathen, and Jason decided to move on out again. They might wring another mile or two out of the day if they hurried. Each man or woman hitched his or her team once more, and off they set.

This time, Jason rode up front with Wash. Not because he wanted to keep an eye on the horizon—Wash was capable of that—but because he wanted to put as much distance as possible between himself and the still-complaining Milcher. As if it was *his* fault that the reverend hadn't replaced that lousy buckle.

He supposed he'd have to hear about it until they reached Tucson. Which, he fervently hoped, would not be on a Sunday.

"You're awful quiet, boy," Wash said.

"Guess so." The comforting creak of leather rode the silence, filling it.

Wash asked, "Want I should shoot us somethin' for supper?"

"We're still eating the steer we butchered last night." And then he quickly added, "Thanks for the offer, though, Wash." It was more than he was getting from most of the others.

Silence again. It began to grow dark, and Jason reined his mount in.

"Enough, Jason?"

"Reckon." They turned their horses around and began to walk back toward the wagons. "Wash, you figure those really were Indians in that dust cloud?"

"Hard tellin'," Wash said with a shrug.

"Well, next time you see something suspicious, you just do exactly what you did today."

Half-hidden beneath his scraggly mustache, Wash's mouth quirked up into a grin. "Even if it puts your Reverend Milcher out a mite?"

"Even if it puts him out a whole bunch. Especially, in fact."

Wash said, "That's the Jason Fury I recollect."

Jason didn't remember having been so, well, *petty* before, but he didn't say anything. He just let it pass, and tried to think kind thoughts about the Milchers. Maybe he was being too hard on them. Well, hard on the reverend, anyway.

In fact, when the new camp circle was formed and everybody was busy uncoupling their draft animals, Jason made a point to go over to Milcher and let him know that Saul Cohen had the hardware and skill to fix his broken harness.

As he had imagined, Milcher turned him down.

The blamed idiot.

26

They traveled down through Apache Pass, into the land that would one day be officially called Arizona but was still a part of New Mexico. The landscape grew more and more rugged, and the Reverend Milcher was overheard to say that the crags and spires of Apache Pass were surely the work of the Devil.

A few miles after they traveled out of it, they came across signs of a massacre. They discovered the burned-to-charcoal remains of a wagon and three charred bodies, which apparently had been tied to the wheels.

Apache arrows were stuck in the low scrub that ringed it.

"Glad Chavez isn't with us anymore," Jason commented when they found a chunk of unburned board with a bit of a sign on it, in Spanish.

"Who?" asked Wash.

"They joined us on the other side of the Sangre de Cristos with Gooding's group," Jason answered. "They got off the trail in Santa Fe."

"Oh. The same Chavez what does the stained glass and ironwork?"

"That's the one."

"Thought they both went back East to pick up stuff for glassmakin'. Him and his brother, I mean."

"They did. Comanches got the brother."

Wash shook his head. "Damned shame. Y'know, I got

half a mind to take off and go buffalo huntin'. Sooner or later, we'll starve the bastards out if we can't get 'em to play nice no other way."

Jason doubted it would make much difference to the Apache. You'd have to kill every steer, goat, hog, rabbit, badger, snake, horse, mule, and burro in the countryside to put a little bit of a rumble in their larcenous stomachs.

He didn't think much of the Apache race. Not as a whole, and not as individuals.

He pulled up his horse and dismounted.

"Whatcha doin'?" asked Wash.

"Better bury these bodies," Jason said, pulling the folding shovel from his saddlebag. The corpses looked like they'd died hideous deaths. Their blackened, shriveled mouths were stretched open in twisted, silent screams. He didn't want Megan or Jenny to see them.

Wash dismounted, too, and found his shovel. "Better hurry, then," he said as he, too, drove his shovel into the hard caliche soil. "Wagons'll be comin' along pretty soon."

Aside from the mystery riders and the hapless Mexicans, they had no more trouble with the Apache, and for this Jason was very glad. They rumbled through Goose Flats, which was little more than a collection of the tents and shacks of miners. They traveled north, the days growing hotter and the nights growing warmer, and came in sight of Tucson and its presidio a few days later.

Jason had the wagons pull directly into the presidio, for safety's sake, and there they set up temporary camp. Jason remembered Tucson as a place where the mosquitos were thick and the swampland even thicker, but it seemed the town had used up most of the old swamp water for irrigation. He didn't even see a mosquito.

By this time, he figured that Matt MacDonald had given up on killing him, since he was still breathing. In fact, he'd only caught a couple glimpses of Matt since Santa Fe. A coward was always a coward, he'd decided.

Megan, on the other hand, was ever present. He'd taken to walking with her in the evenings. Those evenings when it was safe, anyhow.

He'd also explained that he couldn't stay. That he wanted to go back East, to college. To live back East and never see the West again.

She said she understood, but somehow, he had a hard time believing her. He was having an increasingly hard time believing himself.

His pilgrims took full advantage of Tucson, even if they didn't speak any Spanish. Personally, he found it difficult to get around without speaking Spanish, but Wash spoke it fluently, and did the linguistic navigating for him and Saul and Salmon.

Their first stop was Cantina de los Lobos, where Salmon had far too much tequila and Wash practically took a bath in beer, or *cerveza*, as the locals called it. They all partook of the cuisine, which turned out to be enchiladas, enchiladas, and more enchiladas.

By the time they left, Saul and Jason were carrying Salmon between them while Wash staggered along behind, weaving and farting his way down the street.

"Jason Fury!" Jenny scolded when they finally stumbled back into the presidio. "Have you been drinking?"

"Wash and Salmon drank it all up before I had a chance," he said.

Her eyes narrowed, as if she didn't quite believe him. "Well, Megan's been looking for you."

"Figures," he said, and let Salmon slide to the ground.

"Thank you," huffed Saul, who'd been holding up Salmon's other side and was plainly tired.

"Welcome," said Jason. "Where is she, Jenny?"

"Over at our wagon."

"What's wrong?" Jenny seemed nervous and upset, not at all like herself.

But she said, "Nothing. Go see Megan, all right?" And then she turned from him and toward Salmon, on the ground. "Saul, you should have know better than to let him get like this. He's going to feel awful in the morning."

As Jason walked away, he heard Saul say, "Better he should feel awful in the morning than I should have a broken jaw tonight."

When Jason reached the wagon, he called, "Megan?"

Teary-eyed, she emerged from the tail end of the Conestoga and climbed down. She was still dressed, though she had pulled a quilt about her, like a cape.

"What is it?" he asked, suddenly concerned. "What's wrong?"

"It's Matt. I'm so sorry to bother you with this. I mean, seeing as how the two of you are like water and oil."

"What about him?" he asked, without denying her charge. It was common knowledge, after all. "I haven't even seen him, except for a snatch here and there, for days."

"He's in jail, in town, and nobody will go and get him out." She burst into tears, and he pulled her close despite his reservations to the contrary.

"It's all right, Meg, don't cry," he whispered into her setter-red hair. "I'll get him out."

"But it's serious." She wept against his shoulder. "H-he killed someone."

Jason had no words to reply to her. He knew that Matt MacDonald would come to no good, but this was pretty early for him to turn from a schoolyard bully into a cold-blooded killer.

At last, he said, "They're wrong, Megan. I don't believe it. Where is he?"

He took Saul and Wash with him. Wash was sobering up faster than anybody could have expected, and Jason thought they might need him to breach the language barrier.

When they reached the jail, however, the sheriff turned out to be an Irishman named Clancy—or so said the little sign on his desk—and he sure enough had Matthew locked up in a cell. Matt didn't look any too happy about it either. And neither did he act overjoyed to see Jason, Saul, and Wash come in the front door.

"Can I be of assistance to you gents?" asked Clancy, rocking forward with a thump to put all four legs of his chair on the floor.

"As a matter of fact, you can," Jason said with the friendliest smile he could muster. He stuck out his hand. "I'm Jason Fury, sir. Wagon master of the train parked over in the presidio?"

The sheriff shook his hand. "Sheriff Clancy. I heard about you folks. Believe I've got one of your company under custody, as a matter of fact." He nodded toward Matt's cell. "You come to see me about him?"

"What's he charged with?" Jason asked.

"Well, seems he picked himself a fight up at the Purple Garter. Picked it with the wrong fellow, too." Clancy leaned forward and whispered, "Y'know, your boy here isn't too smart. I'd be keepin' him under lock and key if I were you."

Wash farted loudly, then collapsed into a chair. "'Scuse me," he muttered.

Nobody paid him any mind other than Saul, who turned red and cleared his throat.

"How much is his fine?" Jason asked, pretending Megan hadn't so much as breathed the word "murder." He knew the MacDonalds were well fixed—although not so well fixed as they had been before Hamish came tumbling down the mountain—and Matt could pay him back later.

"No fine," said the sheriff. When Jason looked puzzled, he added, "See, he decided to knock out Jose Vasquez, then take a knife to him. The son of Miguel Vasquez? Oh, hell. The Vasquez family's been the big muckety-mucks around here since who laid the rail."

"The big what-whats?" piped up a puzzled Saul. In the corner, Wash let loose another round of gas.

"Well, what's it going to take to get him out of here by morning?" Jason asked.

The sheriff sat down again and folded his arms. "Sorry, boys. Can't help you. Got to go to trial. Unless . . ."

Jason leaned forward. "Unless what?"

"Unless you can get him clean out of the territory. I don't care much for the Vasquez bunch, myself. Old Miguel holds himself pretty damned high, if you ask me. But I think that's going to be tough, considering that your friend here called him a stinking Mex and tossed a near-full spittoon over him before the fight even started."

Jason looked over at Matt, then back at the sheriff. "Aw, crud."

With the still-half-drunken Wash along for linguistic support, Jason and Saul set out for the Purple Garter in search of Miguel Vasquez, father of the murdered boy. Try though they might, however, he was nowhere to be found.

After going to the Purple Garter and four other saloons, they bumped into one of his cronies, a man who swore that Miguel had ridden home after the incident. And that furthermore, his *compadre* Miguel had still been angrier than a sack full of wet bobcats. He'd wanted to lynch Matt right then and there.

From the tone of the speaker, Jason decided that he wouldn't want Miguel mad at *him*. But what could he do? Like it or not, Matt was his responsibility. Additionally, he was Megan's brother.

He had no choice.

He and Wash and Saul went back to the presidio, where Wash passed out, Saul went to be with his family, and after making sure the water barrels were all refilled, Jason went to his wagon, to face Megan and his sister.

He had a feeling they weren't going to be any too keen on his plan. He wasn't, either.

He got them together and urged them inside the wagon, where he joined them.

"Listen up, you two," he began. "I can't get him out before we leave. In fact, I don't think I can get him out at all. Legally, that is. He killed a man in a bar brawl."

Megan's face fell, and Jenny didn't look too good, either. He'd had suspicions that something was going on between Matt and Jenny, but then again, he didn't really want to know. He'd just been hoping he was wrong, but Jenny's face told him otherwise, damn it.

"I'm going to break him out," he said. But he tried to sound as if it didn't even strike him as breaking the law, just as if Matt was his lifelong friend, just as if Jason was invincible.

He sounded a great deal more secure than he felt.

27

At four o'clock, he roused the camp. They were a little cranky about being awakened before the dawn, but he managed to get everybody moving. They started to hitch their teams and eat their breakfasts.

He slipped into town, taking Ward Wanamaker with him. Ward had volunteered, saying that Jason was a fool if he thought anybody, man or women or sheriff, could see him once and forget him, and that was just the way it was.

Ward went into the sheriff's office first, found a groggy deputy on duty, managed to crack him over the head, then called for Jason.

Together, they tied and gagged the luckless deputy, found the key to Matt's cell, and locked up the unconscious deputy in his place.

Matt, who had said nothing during the entire procedure, finally spoke just as they were leaving. And then, only one word. A growl on his face, he looked at Jason and said, "Why?"

"Because you paid my pa to take you to California," Jason said. "Now, shut up."

"Huh?"

"Quiet!"

"Listen, you son of a bitch, if you're gonna—"

Ward stepped between them and grumbled, "If you two are set on killin' each other, I'd suggest you wait till we get clear of town."

They slipped out, the streets still being mostly devoid of people except for the occasional dozing drunkard, and walked quietly toward the presidio. When they reached it, the wagons were ready to go. In fact, Salmon and Saul, both of whom knew what Jason and Ward were up to, had already lined the Conestogas up and started them out the presidio gate.

Jason saw someone waving at him, squinted, and realized it was Jenny.

"Come on," he said, grabbing hold of Matt.

Ward grabbed the other arm, and they fairly dragged Matt, kicking and hollering, to the wagon. Halfway there, Jason had finally had enough. He slugged Matthew on the jaw as hard as he could, and as he'd hoped, Matt crumpled.

"That's better," Ward said.

They dragged Matt's limp body the rest of the way to the wagon, and tossed him up into its bed. Jenny covered him over with quilts—"In case anybody gets nosy," she said—while Megan drove on. Saul had already tacked up Jason and Ward's horses, and they sprang up on them and went immediately to work—Ward with the herd and remuda, and Jason with the wagons—and Jenny ran to drive Salmon Kendall's wagon. Salmon was still passed out in the back.

Saul flagged Jason down when they were about a half mile out of the presidio and asked, "Why didn't you take me along? I never helped in a jailbreak before."

"That's why," Jason said. "Didn't want to start any new habits."

Later that day, while they were slowly working their way north in the shadow of the Santa Rita Mountains, Sheriff Clancy caught up with them. Jason saw him coming and met him at the middle of the caravan.

"Well, what brings you up this way, Sheriff?" Jason asked.

The sheriff reined in his horse next to Jason's. He was not smiling. The opposite, in fact. "I think you know that answer to that, Fury. I want him back. Now."

"What? Who?"

"Don't play games, Fury. I'll search every single wagon in this train if I have to."

Jason propped his hand on his saddle horn and shook his head. "Think you might have a hard time convincing folks to do that, Sheriff, seeing that you're out of your jurisdiction, and also seeing that you arrested one of our most popular members last night. How's Matt doing, by the way? Have you set a trial date?"

Clancy glared at him.

"I'd like to know," Jason went on. "A few of us would like to come back for the hearing. You know, make sure everything's on the up and up?"

Clancy said, "Cut the horseshit, Fury. You and I both know you've got him."

Jason's eyes widened. "We do?"

But Clancy was adamant. "You know damn well that MacDonald broke outta jail early this mornin'. Just before your wagon train pulled out. That's too big a coincidence, Fury."

Jason sighed. "Well, then, I guess we've got a problem, Sheriff. Now, I wouldn't mind you searching my wagons. Wouldn't mind it a bit, personally, although I can't speak for some of the ladies in our party. But see, I've got to get these people to California in a hurry, and we already lost several days trying to get across the Canadian River during a thunderstorm."

"That's not my problem."

"I think it is."

They sat there, their horses dancing nervously between them while the wagons slowly passed. And then at last, Sheriff Clancy turned his horse and rode back toward Tucson, without a word.

Jason sat there on Cleo, watching him go and thanking the Lord for allowing the sheriff to buy into his bluff. Especially when it was done to protect a cowardly murdering jackass like Matt MacDonald.

Two days later, they swung west again along the Old Mormon Trail and entered a flat, endless plain of desert scrub and blooming cactus called El Despoblado, a wild, ummapped part of the territory. They made steady progress, although Jason posted several men as scouts. They looked in every direction for Apache, who could use the low cover in their favor.

The talk around the campfire, in the evenings, was turning toward farming, and most of the men agreed that this wide plain would make for fine crops. All it needed was water.

Jason pointed out that it would also most likely produce trouble with the Apache, but folks were too excited about the land to listen to him. Additionally, it had been a while since they'd had Indian trouble, and they seemed to have pushed the reality of it away.

Jason pointed out that there were no trees, and therefore, no shade.

Saul said that they could plant some.

Jason pointed out that the Milchers already had purchased land in California.

The Reverend Milcher remarked that he could get his money back, and didn't his flock here need him?

All of this was pointless, Jason figured. There was no water, period. Of course, there was water underground here and there, but he didn't mention it. He just wanted to get these folks across the Colorado River and into California.

But the next day, they came to a small stream thickly lined with cottonwood trees for as far as the eye could see. The Reverend Milcher proclaimed it a sign from on high, akin to manna in the desert. Privately, Saul told Jason, "I wish he'd stick to his half of the Holy Book."

Jason pointed out that in California, trees had already been planted, and towns—hungry for new citizens—had already been founded. And he was fairly sure that the rivers and streams there ran year round, something he couldn't say for Arizona streams.

Salmon Kendall looked up. "They disappear?" He had been keeping company with Carrie English of late, and sat beside her at the campfire, whittling a little model of Rags for Chrissy.

"They still flow," Jason said, "but they do it underground. Least, that's what I'm told. It'll be pretty hard to irrigate your fields when there's no aboveground water to do it with."

"I've seen it done," piped up Ezekial Morton, the senior member of their group, and usually the most taciturn.

That captured Milcher's attention, and he was on Ezekial like a duck on a June bug. "Where, Brother Morton? How?"

"In Tucson," Morton replied. "While you young bucks were out painting the town, I took a little sightseeing tour. They got them big, deep wells dug down there. Got a sort of augerlike contraption in the center of 'em that brings up the water, and two mules run it. Day and night, the man told me." He scratched at his beard. "Course, I suppose they change the mules out two or three times a day. . . ."

"Well, there you go!" exclaimed the reverend. "We'll build one of those for the dry season!"

Jason shook his head. "You know, the only reason I can think of for you folks staying here instead of going on to California and some sort of civilization is that you'll have to buy land in California, and here it's free for the taking."

The resounding calls of "That's right!" and "Yes!" and "Durn tootin'!" almost knocked Jason off the hay bale he was sitting on. These people were not only cheap, they were crazy.

Wash, apparently the only other sane one in the bunch, said, "What you gonna build them auger things out of? Cottonwood?"

"That's correct, sir!" Milcher answered confidently.

Wash shook his head and clucked his tongue. "Don't you know you can't kill cottonwood? Hell, fence posts made from it sprout in the ground and give you a fence fulla trees in no time! Cain't imagine what kinda bushy nonsense you'd get if you was to stick 'em down a well!"

"He's right," said Jason.

"We can get other kinds of wood," Salmon Kendall said. "And we've got our wagons. There's plenty of wood in them, and I'll bet it isn't cottonwood."

A murmur of agreement spread over the group.

Jason sighed. He couldn't fight them on it. He said, "All right. Those who want to stay here, can. Those who want to go on to California, I'll lead them. Anybody?"

He looked out over the crowd. There wasn't one taker among them. Against his better wishes, he said, "Fine. I'll stay and help you get your town started, then. I owe you that much."

The Reverend Milcher stood straight up and raised his fist. "Hoorah!" he shouted. And then most everyone rose as one man, and echoed his cry.

"Tomorrow," he said, once everyone had quieted down, "I shall consecrate this land. And we shall also name our new town."

"Well," Matt MacDonald said, stepping from the shadows, "it looks like decent grazing land, anyhow."

"I vote we name it for Jason's daddy!" said Salmon.

"A wise idea," Saul said.

The Reverend Milcher frowned. It looked as if this wasn't going the way he had expected. "Is that a second?"

"What else would it be?" Saul responded.

"Very well, then. All those in favor?"

The small crowd thundered, "Aye!"

Hopefully, Milcher added, "Opposed?"

Not one word was uttered.

Except by a puzzled Jason, who asked, "You're going to name the town Jedediah?"

Saul slapped his shoulder. "No, boy! Fury! And we'll build it right here, right where we are standing."

Heads nodded all round.

Jason was beaten, and he knew it. These fools would try to build their town right here, and the newly christened Fury would fall to the Apache or just plain dry up and blow away.

He said, "If you're set on it."

28

Jason and Megan were strolling around the inside of the circled wagons, because Jason didn't want to take a chance on Megan getting snakebit out there in the brush and grass. Since Tucson, he had given up on trying to keep their mutual attraction private, and they strolled openly, arms linked.

"You don't like this idea, do you, Jason?" she asked. "The whole thing about the town, I mean."

"No," he said firmly.

"But why not?"

He looked down at her. "Weren't you listening earlier?"

"Yes, but I thought you were just trying to paint the worst possible picture to dissuade the Reverend Milcher from giving up his land in California. And let the others know that it won't be easy."

Jason didn't say anything.

"We know it won't be easy, Jason. But we're here, we have water and land—land forever! And it's just here for the taking!"

"You realize you're probably going to build right smack in the center of somebody's range land?"

"But nobody owns the range, Jason."

"True. But some people like to think they do. And then there are the Apache."

She gave a little sigh. "They haven't bothered us yet."

"Not yet. But that doesn't mean they won't. We're sitting in the middle of their home range, too."

She looked down for some time, while they walked the length of three wagons. "You're not going to stay, are you?"

"Not any longer than I have to." He felt bad about leaving her, but he had to tell the truth. He was leaving eventually. "I'll stay long enough to help get the first buildings up and make sure you're settled in, but then I'm going."

Megan turned her head away and whispered, "All right. I understand, I guess. Will you take Jenny with you?"

He hadn't ever thought of *not* taking Jenny. "Yes."

"Does she know about this? She's pretty stuck on my brother, you know."

Jason stiffened. He hadn't wanted to know about it, had tried to ignore it, push it from his mind. And now here it was. He said, "Tough."

Megan stopped walking, and he stopped, too. Her hands, curled into fists, were cocked on her hips. "Tough? That's all you have to say?"

He tried to save it by saying, "What I mean is that it's going to be tough on her. But she's young. What does she know yet? And Matthew doesn't strike me as the type to want to settle down."

She set her pretty jaw. Through clenched teeth, she said, "And I guess you don't strike me as that type, either."

"But Megan—"

"Good night, Jason," she said before she turned and ran for the wagon she shared with Jenny.

"Saul? Saul!"

"Yes, Jason, what is it?" Saul looked up from his work, which, at the present, was digging a hole.

"What's the hole for?"

Saul shrugged. "For a well, you dig a hole."

Jason grinned despite himself. "I think maybe you'd better start again, about twenty, twenty-five yards over. You're right in the middle of the trail. What are you digging it for, anyway?"

"Why, the town's water supply! For when the stream dries up."

This time, Jason couldn't hold back his laugh. He said, "Saul, you'd best make it farther than that, then. If we're going to grow up an entire town around your well, we'd best leave it room enough to grow without every wagon train coming west going right through somebody's front garden."

Saul nodded. "Again, wisdom beyond his years . . ."

"And get somebody to help you," Jason called over his shoulder as he walked away. He had other fish to fry.

Everybody seemed to be of the same mind as Saul in thinking that nobody would ever again use this trail. The wagons were still circled smack on it, with the shallow trail ruts running right through the circle.

Actually, this gave Jason a modicum of hope. Other trains would come through here, and could pick up those who became dissatisfied with their choice to stay. There was a back door, after all.

But folks had already begun setting up shop, right where their rigs sat. Canvas wagon covers were untied and pulled out and staked up for shade, just like Olympia Morelli's was each night to make the cook tent. People were spreading out, freeing up possessions they'd kept squirreled away since the start of their journey.

He was looking for Megan, hoping to clear up their little misunderstanding of the previous night, but was told by Ward Wanamaker that she was gone. And his horse, too!

"Yeah, Matt was headin' off to scout a good place to headquarter a ranch," Ward said. "Megan went with him, and your sister, too. She took your Cleo. Said you wouldn't mind."

Actually, he did mind quite a bit. If Matt wanted to wander around on the plain and act as Apache bait, that was his choice. But he had no business taking the girls with him.

Jason pulled a horse from the remuda, borrowed a saddle and bridle, and made ready to go and bring them back. "Which way did they head?" he asked Ward, as he swung up into the saddle.

Ward pointed. "Southeast. They were followin' the creek. You want I should ride along, Jason? Wash is right over there, too. You might want a couple'a extra guns."

"Yeah." Jason nodded curtly. "Be glad of your company, Ward."

The men spotted the Apache before the Apache spotted them. There were two braves, and they seemed to be trailing somebody. Probably Matt and the girls, because they kept to the cottonwoods along the stream.

Wash pulled out his rifle and started to take aim, but Jason shot out an arm and shoved the barrel aside. "No," he whispered. "Let's see if we can take care of this without any bloodshed."

"But they's only Apache!" Wash hissed, disappointed.

"You shoot two, and you'll have two hundred down here looking for them. And finding the train."

Wash swore under his breath, but shoved his rifle back into its boot. If Ward had any feelings one way or the other, they didn't show on his face.

The Apache had stopped, and so did the men. At a

signal from Jason, the men dismounted. Jason, the only one tall enough to see over the slightly rolling scrub and grass, kept the Indians in sight.

"What?" Wash said. "What do you see?"

Jason shook his head. "I figure that Matt and the girls've stopped up there, somewhere. The Apache are either just waiting them out, or looking for a chance to attack. Or, hell, maybe they don't think it's worth it for a kid and two girls. . . ."

"Worth what?" Ward asked.

"Worth possibly getting shot." Jason kept his eyes on the Indians. They were still mounted, and he could make out their heads and shoulders. "They'll have to have seen that Matt's armed. And if I know Jenny, she's got Papa's shotgun on her."

He just hoped that if she saw those braves on their trail, she'd hold off on blasting them. While they stood there, he ran scenario after scenario through his mind, but all of them ended in blood. Mostly theirs.

At last, he quietly said, "Mount up, boys."

"What you thinkin', Jason?" Wash asked, his eyebrows knitting and relaxing, then knitting again.

Ward, jumpy as a cat in a room full of rockers, said, "Yeah, what?"

"We're gonna charge those Indians, men. Charge 'em full out, yelling and yelping and hollering. There are three of us and two of them, and they know there are more of us ahead of them. What I figure to do is split them off to the east at high speed, then pick up Matt and the girls and hightail it back to camp."

He didn't wait for either of them to respond. He just kicked his horse and took off, screaming at the top of his lungs, and screaming some more.

Ward and Wash followed him, thank the Lord. They all three hooted and hollered at full volume, and the

Indians, shocked and surprised, did exactly what he'd hoped they'd do. They took off at a gallop, heading east over the prairie.

And not one single shot was fired by either party. Jason was proud of that.

The three kept up their hollering until they came in sight of Matt and the girls. Matt was on his feet, trying to see what all the noise was about.

Jenny and Megan had taken shelter behind some weedy cottonwoods at the timber's edge. Jenny had her shotgun raised and ready.

"Don't shoot, Jenny!" Jason called, and they came out of hiding immediately.

"What the hell are you doing, Fury?" Matt demanded. The remains of a picnic, hastily abandoned, were scattered at his feet.

"Saving your butt from Apache," Jason said, and then ordered the girls up on their horses. Matt remained where he stood, clenching and unclenching his fists.

"They're going to come back, MacDonald," Jason said. "No two ways about it. I'd get out of here fast if I were you."

Jason took off the other way—Wash, Ward, and the girls behind him—before Matt had his foot in the stirrup. He started his horse running while he was still trying to gain his second stirrup.

Jason would have found it funny, but he was too busy trying to keep an eye on the girls, watch the east for returning Indians, and guide his horse back to the circle of wagons. When they came skidding in, Jason leapt from the saddle and tossed his reins to Ward, then immediately yanked Jenny down from Cleo's saddle.

"Jason!" she cried.

"What were you thinking?" he demanded. "Don't you know you could have been killed? Or worse?"

When she just stared at him, mouth open, he pushed

her away and began hollering, shouting, "Apache, everybody! On your guard!"

Folks grabbed their guns, tucked their children away, dropped whatever they'd been doing before, and waited.

An hour passed before Jason allowed them to let down their guard, but he still assigned Ward and Wash to keep watch.

The people under his care might think he was crazy, but he didn't care. He was still responsible for them.

And they were, by God, going to keep breathing so long as he was around, whether they liked it or not.

29

Night fell and the Indians still hadn't returned. Saul and Salmon and Milt had managed to dig deep enough to find water. Salmon immediately threw his hat in the air and climbed up out of the hole, certain that their work was done.

But Saul knew they'd have to go deeper. The stream was running now and the water level was high. It would go lower. How much lower, he didn't know. All he knew was that he had forgotten how much he hated well-digging.

Saul also knew that Milt Billings had been hired by Jedediah to care for their livestock and help them across the western expanse, but somehow, Saul didn't believe that Jedediah could have known Billings very well. The whole day long, Milt had complained about Jason seeing Indians where there weren't any.

As far as Saul was concerned, if Jason said there were Apache out there, there were Apache. No two ways about it. And he found his anger with Milt slowly coming to a boil. First off, the ground was too hard. Well, they were all three having to dig it, weren't they?

The next complaint on Milt's list was that Jason had taken Milt's horse when he galloped off into the scrub, and when he'd brought him back, he hadn't even walked him out.

Well, Saul had seen Ward Wanamaker walking out

four horses while they were all arming themselves for the supposed Apache attack, which, he was extremely glad hadn't come.

By the time they crawled up out of that hole, the usually peaceable Saul was ready to whack Milt Billings over the head with a shovel.

But he didn't.

As the three of them sat there, dangling their legs over the edge and watching the water level slowly rise, Saul's boys came out to join them. David, the oldest at ten, said very formally, "Good evening, Father," and helped himself to a little square of ground next to Saul. He dangled his legs over the edge, too. Jacob, eight, and Abraham, six, came next, and both tried to sit on Saul's lap at the same time. Unfortunately, Saul didn't have enough lap, and scooted the larger Jacob to his other side.

"Mother says dinner will be ready in a half hour," David said, then made a face.

"What? You don't like what we're having?"

"Mrs. Jameson gave canned beets again." His voice turned to a whisper. "Even Mr. Cow won't eat them!"

Saul smiled. "Well, we'll see what can be done, David."

The boy visibly relaxed.

"If he was my kid," said Milt, "he'd eat 'em whether he liked 'em or not."

The hairs on the back of Saul's neck went up. "Lucky for him, he is not yours."

"Don't get uppity. All's I meant was that out here, you gotta eat what you're given, when you're given it. 'Cause you ain't likely to be given much of anything again."

"Speak for yourself. I will see to my own."

"Stop it, you two!" said Salmon, just as the alarm rose.

Wash Keough, atop the Kendall wagon, shouted, "Apache! Everybody in! Apache!"

Saul scooped up his boys and ran for the wagons, with Salmon hard on his heels.

"I thought Indians weren't supposed to attack this close to night," huffed Saul as he slid down next to Jason, rifle in hand.

"Don't believe everything you read," was all Jason said. Jenny was beside him, ready to reload.

Rachael, having secreted the boys in the bottom of their wagon, joined Saul.

"Sorry if your meal is ruined, Rachael," Jason said. He could see the cloud of dust rising, now, growing nearer.

"It will do the stew good to wait a little," she replied stoically. "And Olympia had already taken the biscuits off the fire."

Jason tossed a box of cartridges toward Saul. "In case you run out."

But Saul was staring out at something much closer than the approaching cloud of dust. "Dear God," he whispered. "It's Milt! He fell in!"

Jason shifted his gaze and saw the well that Saul had been digging, and saw Milt trying to pull his way out. The water must have risen, and it looked like he was having a hard time gaining any purchase on the muddy walls.

"Stay put, Milt!" Jason shouted. The cloud was getting closer. "Keep your head down!"

"I keep it down, I'm gonna drown!"

Jason stood up, muttering "Damn!" and made a run for Milt.

He heard his sister shouting behind him to come back,

but he was already halfway there. When he reached Milt, the dust cloud was almost upon him, and he was vaguely surprised that the Indians weren't screaming war cries, weren't screaming anything at all. But he reached down and gripped Milt's hand, and yanked with all his might. Milt came up out of that well like a catfish on a hook, and scrambled back toward the wagons on Jason's heels, spraying well water as he went.

They both skidded inside just as the forms of the men within the cloud could be made out.

Not Apache.

Not Indians at all.

The party reined in about twenty feet from the circled wagons, and a single rider emerged from the yellow mist of dust still surrounding the rest of his comrades. "Hello the wagons!" he called. He was dressed in an ordinary way, with Levi's, boots, and a flannel shirt. And he had a badge pinned to his belt.

Jason stood up. "Who's that out there? Be careful, there's a newly dug well about five yards from where you're sitting that horse."

"Thanks for the warning, friend. I'm Deputy U.S. Marshal Bill Gordon, with a party of deputies. We've been out after Juan Alba and his band. Finally picked up tracks, and here we are. Good thing, too, because we were about to lose sight of 'em."

"How many men you got with you, Marshal?" Jason called.

"Fifteen."

Jason leaned toward Rachael. "Can we feed fifteen extra?"

She nodded in the affirmative and Saul said, "They can have David's beets."

A muffled, "Hooray!" came from deep within the Cohens' wagon.

"Come on in, Marshal," Jason called with a wave of his hand. "We were just about to have some dinner."

Nearby, Jason heard a still-sodden Milt grumble, "Apaches, my butt."

There was plenty of stew to go around, and one of Marshal Gordon's men gobbled up David's detested beets and asked for more. Mrs. Jameson was visibly pleased, but offered no seconds, which came as a surprise to no one.

While they ate, Gordon regaled them all with the flamboyant—and sometimes grisly—exploits of Juan Alba, or, as the marshal frequently referred to him, the Scourge of the Borderlands. The kids, from little Constantine Morelli and Abraham Cohen to Sammy Kendall and Seth Milcher, were transfixed, and Gordon played to his audience.

Jason had the feeling that this Alba was someone akin to the outlaws of Kansas and Missouri—blamed for most of the deeds done by other gangs, whether they were in the area or not.

Milt Billings was still drying out beside the fire, and still grousing about getting dunked in the well, and the Apache alarm being raised, and having hired on in the first place.

Finally, Jason couldn't stand it any longer—he was enjoying Gordon's stories, too—and quietly stood up. He walked over to Milt and said, "You can leave any time, you know. Nothing's holding you here."

"I just might," Billings said. "These people are daft! Wanting to build a town in the middle of nowhere, in the middle of Apache country!"

"I agree with you, Milt. But this is the place they picked."

Milt picked up his socks from the edge of the fire and shook them out to see if they were dry. He was barefoot, because he'd propped his boots upside down on sticks a little further from the flames. "Well, it sure ain't my choice for a quiet neighborhood."

"Like I said, Milt, the door's open. Marshal Gordon's pulling out in the morning. You can go with him."

"Where's he headed?"

"Prescott."

Milt appeared to mull this over for a moment, and then said, "I'll take the last of my wages tonight, if you don't mind, Jason."

Jason paid him on the spot. He was sorry to lose Milt's gun, but that was all.

"You were horrible to Jenny this afternoon," Megan said as they walked around the inside of the circled wagons.

"I should have been horrible to you, too," Jason said. As if he could be horrible to Megan. "You were in real danger. Those two braves were eyeing you. Tonight, by rights, Matt would be dead and you and Jenny would be Mrs. Kills-with-a-Spear or something."

Megan snorted out a little laugh. They spoke quietly, for most of the camp was asleep. The sound of Salmon Kendall's snores made a steady, rhythmic bass note in the background, overridden by the calls of night birds and the rustle of soft wind that played the brush and scrub like a harp.

Well, a very dry and brittle harp.

"Well, I'm glad you came and saved us. I don't want to be Mrs. Kills-with-a-Spear."

He looked down at her, this setter-haired, elfin thing who had stolen his heart, and he was tempted, so tempted to just throw his future aside, just chuck it all and promise to stay with her, ask her to marry him, to be with him always.

But he fought off the temptation.

He walked her back to the wagon, then relieved Wash of sentry duty.

He had a lot of thinking to do.

30

Summer came, and under the blistering heat, the pioneers built homes and businesses from the adobe bricks Jason showed them how to make from dirt, water, and straw. Saul dug his well deeper and deeper and deeper, and eventually the stream dried up.

Matt MacDonald began construction of his new ranch house, several miles south of Fury. He had grand dreams, all right, and he labored out there night and day with no one but Gil Collins, whom he had hired away from Jason, to help him.

Jason oversaw the town proper. He and Ward and Salmon and several other men helped Saul build his hardware store, with living quarters on a second floor. They used the beds and side timbers of both Saul's wagons to floor the second story, and chopped down ten enormous cottonwoods to make the exposed beams of the ceilings.

Somewhere along the line, they had mutually decided to all work on one man's home or business until it was finished, and then move on, as a gang, to the next. It worked fine, and in this way they also built the Nordstroms' mercantile and a livery and got started on a house for Salmon Kendall, who had recently wed Carrie English and taken on Chrissy and Rags as his own, too. Chrissy seemed to be getting along famously with Sammy and Peony, who enjoyed having a little sister. They had taken to Carrie, too, although it was obvious that the loss of their mother still cut deep.

Around Saul's well they built a low wall, put an A-frame over it for reeling buckets up and down, and it sat in the center of a large patio in the very center of what was becoming the town of Fury.

Around the perimeter of this "town square," the buildings slowly rose here and there, like the scattered teeth of an old man. In between, there sat wagons not yet evacuated or abandoned, their canvases spread and staked like open-air tents.

"It's really turning into something," Jason said to Jenny, one night after the work was done and they finished their supper.

"You didn't think it would?" Jenny asked him. "I always knew they'd make something wonderful."

Jenny, now sixteen, had bloomed over these last few months. Her blond hair was streaked quite fetchingly by the sun, her complexion glowed, and she had grown a half inch taller and filled out. She was no longer the gawky colt of a girl he remembered, but a beautiful young woman. The realization came as something of a shock to him.

"You always had more faith than anybody I ever knew, baby sister," he said.

"Papa used to call me that, too."

"I know." He put an arm around her shoulders and gave her a little hug.

"You're thinking about leaving, aren't you?"

Once again, he was surprised. He hadn't known it was that obvious. "Yes, I guess I am."

"Then you'll go alone, Jason. I'm not going with you."

He stared at her, lost for words.

"I'm going to marry Matt MacDonald and stay here and raise babies, horses, and cattle, in that order."

This time, he found the words. "No! No, you're not!

You're coming with me. You're going to live where there are no Indians, no bandits, where people can act like people and not animals, Jenny. And you're going to marry some nice, civilized, educated man, not a fool like Matt MacDonald!"

She slapped his face so hard it rattled his teeth. "I am too going to marry Matt!"

"Jenny, has he even asked?"

"He's not a fool!" She turned and ran to the wagon before he could think to say anything. She was probably hurrying to repeat everything he'd said to Megan.

Great, just great.

And he stood there, rubbing his cheek and wondering what in the world had possessed him to choose those particular words. He probably shouldn't have called Matt a fool, for one thing, although that was the nicest tag he could think of to hang on him. Stupid, dumb son of a bitch would have been closer to it.

And then he began to think about what she'd said. Raise babies and horses and cattle.

In that order?

He marched after her, hands and jaw clenched. If that bastard had been at her, he'd kill him.

He reached the wagon and climbed up onto the seat. Turning backward to face the cargo area, he shouted, "Jenny!"

Two faces popped up from beneath the quilts: Megan's and Jenny's. Megan looked surprised, but Jenny just looked mad.

"Jenny, has Matt MacDonald . . . has he . . . ?"

Megan cried, "Jason Fury!"

But Jason only had eyes for his sister. He forced himself to spit out the words. "Has he got you in a family way, Jenny?"

Jenny looked completely shocked. "Jason! Of course not! How dare you even *think* that I—"

Jason closed his eyes. "Thank God," he whispered, and slipped away.

The next morning, after talking to Jenny again and making something of a peace with her, Jason made ready to leave. He'd resigned himself to follow Jenny's wishes. After all, she was grown, and he couldn't exactly kidnap her to bring her along, could he? He had decided to go up to San Francisco instead of back East. It was a big town, and a rich one. Surely they had colleges up there, too, and plenty of opportunities for an enterprising young man to work his way through school.

Also, it meant that he'd be closer to Jenny.

And Megan.

Maybe, after he got settled and got some education under his belt, he could come back for Megan. If she'd have him. If she hadn't already married.

"Stop it, you peckerwood," he muttered as he saddled up Cleo. If he didn't, he'd talk himself into staying. That was the last thing he wanted to do.

So he managed to pull his mind away from Megan and set it on a more useful purpose—plotting his course to San Francisco.

He figured to head due west, to the coast, and then ride straight north. He'd never exactly taken that route before—his total experience of the road west was one trip over the southern route when he was fourteen and one trip over the Oregon Trail when he was twelve, both of which had been overseen by his father. But he figured that if he did as he had planned, he couldn't miss San Francisco.

He heard footsteps behind him. "Jason?" It was Megan. She said, "You're really going, then. Jenny told me, but I didn't believe her. I thought you'd stay until the whole town was built, anyway."

"You've got a good enough start on everything," he replied. "And you know towns. It'll never be finished." They had picked up four more wagonloads of folks just last week. He tried not to look at her, but then she put her hand on his arm, and he turned toward her as if her touch had magnetized him.

"Jason," she whispered, her eyes brimming with tears.

He kissed her. He kissed her hard and long, knowing that he might never be allowed this privilege again.

And then abruptly, he let go of her, leaving her swaying, and mounted his mare. His throat was so thick that he had no words to say good-bye. He simply nodded, his heart full, then rode away.

Roughly twenty minutes after Jason bade good-bye to Megan and rode west, Matthew was awakened from his siesta by Gil Collins, whom he'd hired to help him build his house.

"What?" he said, cranky with the heat and tired from the work.

Gil hurried down from the ladder, which leaned against the partially finished second story, and started running for the horses. "Riders!" he shouted as Matt climbed to his feet. "Comin' fast from the south."

Matt stopped and cocked his fists on his hips. "I suppose these are more of Fury's imaginary Apache?"

Gil leapt into the saddle, grabbed Matt's pinto by the reins, and brought him to Matt at a hard trot. "Not imaginary. Look." Then he tossed Matt the pinto's reins and lit out toward Fury at a dead gallop.

"Coward," Matt grumbled under his breath, but he swung up on the horse, just to get a higher vantage point.

He looked toward the south.

Through clenched teeth, he said, "Damn it!" then lashed the pinto.

He had only loped about thirty yards before the first arrow sank into his arm like a hot branding iron. He didn't look back. He was afraid to see what was chasing him, although the first whoops were just now reaching his ears.

He hunkered lower in the saddle and dug his spurs into the pinto's flanks.

His pinto was fast, faster even than Jason's Cleo or any of his father's Morgans. He slowly gained on Gil, who was racing for town, and then drew even with him. He glimpsed the fear on Gil's face and saw him draw his revolver.

Gil began to fire just after Matt passed him.

In Fury, Saul was the first one to hear the shots. "Listen!" he said to the others. "Do you hear?"

Randall Nordstrom furrowed his brow. "That's out Matt's way. You think they're hunting rabbits?"

"Too close," said Salmon. He scurried up the ladder to the window of Nordstrom's second floor, then stood up in the window casing to get a better look.

"What?" asked Saul.

Salmon came halfway down the ladder, then jumped the rest of the way. "Apache! And Matt and Gil are ridin' in, hell-bent for leather!"

Saul started to yell, "Circle the wagons!" then remembered that half their wagons were broken up or staked out. Thank God the Mortons had taken most of the livestock up north with them, to where they were building their houses.

Salmon was yelling, "Apache! Get your arms! Apache!" and Randall Nordstrom was already upstairs, in his store, pointing a rifle out the glassless window.

Saul ran to the northwest edge of the square and the ammunition wagon, which hadn't yet been unloaded, and grabbed a couple handfuls of cartridge boxes. One, he tossed up to Randall. The others, he passed out to the men who were already running to Fury's southern perimeter.

To his side, Rachael ran out the front door of his store. He saw her and he called, "Rachael, the children?"

"Under their beds. Saul, come now!"

He ran for her just as Matt MacDonald thundered between them. Saul didn't have to think twice. "Matt!" he cried as the boy leapt off his horse.

Saul could see he was wounded. "Come!" He waved frantically. He could hear the Indians now, hear them growing close with every second. Already, the men on the southern side of the square were firing. "Matt, come here! Come inside!"

Gil Collins came into town just as Saul helped Matt through the door. Gil had taken an arrow deep in his back, and was slumped over his horse's neck.

Saul flagged down the tired horse, slid Gil's limp body to the ground, and slapped the horse on the rump before he dragged Gil inside and bolted the door behind them.

Catty-corner across the town square, to the south, the men opened fire.

31

Jason turned to take one last look at the distant horizon, one last look at the land in which he'd left his sister and his love and, he admitted, his friends.

But something was wrong with the horizon. Above the line of trees that followed the creek there rose a thin, moving line of dust. And it was moving toward Fury.

His first thought was Apache, but then he got a grip, telling himself that it was likely another false alarm. Probably just another federal marshal, out on another fool's errand.

But he turned around anyway, and headed back where he'd come from. He urged the palomino into a soft lope. You couldn't be too careful, he supposed, and he could always leave again in the morning.

Maybe he could get Jenny to make him up some beef sandwiches for the road, if they slaughtered a steer tonight.

The sound of the battle came to Ezekial Morton, two miles north of Fury. "Zachary!" he called to his older brother. "There's trouble in town!"

Ezekial's daughters, Europa and Electa, both big, strapping girls, looked up from their chore of mixing adobe and making bricks, glad for the distraction, and joined their father and uncle.

"Mama!" Europa called to the house, or anyway, what there was of it at this point. "Mama, bring Aunt Suzannah!"

Suzannah and Eliza came from the house, and the whole family stood there, listening to the distant gunfire. Ezekial thought it sounded like Independence Day. If you were British.

He suddenly felt cold all over, despite the heat.

"Should we go back?" Electa asked. She was always the optimist, his Electa.

"And do what?" her uncle Zachary said, stroking his beard. "We are best to stay here. Suzannah, put out that cook fire. Now. It makes too much smoke."

Suzannah obeyed as fast as her aged legs would move her.

"Eliza, darlin', you and the girls go inside, too," Ezekial said. "Arm yourselves. Zachary and I will keep watch."

Zachary cocked a grizzled brow. "We will?"

"Yes, Zach. We will."

"Well, I think I'll have a pipe, then." He held out his tobacco pouch. "Care to try my blend?"

"Don't mind if I do."

Jason slowed up on the far side of the creek and made his way through the trees on foot, leading his horse. The sounds and cries were unmistakable, now. This was not an errant marshal. These were Apache on a raid. It sounded like a passel of them, too.

Still on the other side of the creek, hidden from the attackers, he made his way upstream—or what would have been upstream, if there'd been any water flowing—until he was at the far north edge of the town.

Then he mounted his horse, wove through the cottonwoods, and at their edge, suddenly raced forward toward the ammo wagon. He knew the men had to be running low by now.

The Apache were so preoccupied by the settlers, who seemed to have primarily grouped at the south end of town, that they didn't notice him, and he grabbed up all the ammunition he could carry in a gunnysack, left Cleo behind the wagon, and hurried along the fronts of the buildings on the east side of the square, the sack of ammo in one hand and his gun in the other.

Still, no one saw him until a door suddenly opened and he found himself yanked inside. He turned his gun on the person that had dragged him in, then saw it was Saul.

"You came back?" Saul asked, surprised.

"Looks like," Jason answered, then handed the ammunition bag over. While Saul dug through it, Jason spied Gil in the corner, hurt bad. He didn't need to ask what had happened. Instead, he asked, "Where's Morelli?"

Saul motioned with his head. "South wall. Matt MacDonald's upstairs. He galloped in about two shakes before the Apache."

Muttering, "It figures," he snatched back the sack. "Got everything you need?"

"Yes."

"Then get back to it. I've got to get down to the men." He stood up, staying well back from the windows, and turned for the door, then hesitated. "Where are your boys?"

"Upstairs. Rachel put them under their beds."

"Bring them down. The first thing the Apache will do, if we can't turn 'em back, is set fire to the roofs."

"What? But how?"

"Flaming arrows." Jason shut the door between them.

What he saw didn't hearten him much. The new livery was already on fire. Flames licked at the cottonwood roof, bellowed from the windows, and ran the length of the new cottonwood fence. It billowed black smoke.

"Well, I suppose that'll keep 'em from sprouting," he muttered as, hunkered low, he made his way toward the battle. Above him, in front of Nordstrom's, he heard a shot ring out and looked up just in time to see the muzzle of a rifle withdraw.

"That you, Randall?" he called.

"*Yah!*" came the shouted answer. Jason dug through the bag until he found .44 rimfire cartridges, then hollered, "Catch! Ammo!"

Nordstrom's head and one arm popped through the opening, and he snatched up the box of cartridges Jason threw.

Jason heard his muted "Thank you!" as he scuttled down the street.

But somebody had seen him, for just then three Apache arrows buried themselves in the dirt at his feet.

He pulled his gun and fired back, although he didn't know exactly who to fire at. Any Indian would do at this point.

They had come around, between, and over the southern buildings now, and were attacking from both sides of them. Jason shot two braves that were hacking at the roof of Milcher's new church. He didn't know who shot the other one, but all three tumbled to the ground like rag dolls.

He was rewarded for this by an Apache arrow that sank into his thigh. It stung like hell, but all he could do for the time being was break off the shaft. Morelli would have to cut it out. He already knew he couldn't push it through because he could feel it scraping the bone.

Some of the Apache had guns, but as far as he could tell, they didn't have any repeaters. Yet.

Limping, he slid around the corner of the building,

into an alley, and across it to peek around the corner of the wagon parked at its side.

The savages were swarming over the buildings now. He knew he'd never get any ammunition through to his people. And then he suddenly remembered Salmon Kendall. Salmon Kendall was the only one with an old rifle, one that took powder and ball. And in that sack, he'd put balls and power for Salmon.

He had an idea. It was dangerous, and it might not work at all, but it was all he had at the moment.

He ducked back into the shadows of the wagon's undercarriage and quickly unraveled three burlap strings from the bag, which he proceeded to braid together, just as he had braided his sister's hair when she was younger.

He affixed one end of the braid to the bag, and then pulled out the small keg of powder, the smallest one he'd been able to find in the ammo wagon. He opened it and shook half its contents out over everything else in the sack, and also over the length of his makeshift fuse.

He hoped it would work. He'd never done it before, never even seen it done. He said a brief prayer, reclosed the half-full keg and stuck it back inside the bag, then lit the fuse.

It burned faster than he'd expected, and he had to toss it in a hurry. Even so, in that brief moment he was exposed, he took another arrow to the shoulder, and thought, *What am I? A pincushion?*

He jumped back into the shadow of the wagon again and waited. Nothing happened. *Damn it!* Either the quickness of the throw had blown out the fuse, or the concussion when it hit had knocked the fuse free of the sack. Either way, his makeshift bomb hadn't gone off.

He crawled underneath the wagon, and on his belly, he took aim and shouted, "Take cover, men!" He fired. And missed.

He hit it with the second shot.

The bag exploded in a thick haze of black smoke, and bullets zinged every which way. Since the Indians were out in the open, it did them, by far, the most damage. Bodies fell right and left, scattered in piles like autumn leaves, and the wood over Jason's head was splintered by three wild slugs.

Fortunately, most of the townsmen had heard and heeded his warning, and jumped back inside what few buildings there were. He still heard shots being fired inside the buildings, their sound muffled as opposed to the bright *zings* of the ordnance from the bag.

Blood flowed in a river from Jason's leg. He felt weak, and with the last of his strength, he attempted to tie off the leg with his bandanna. That was the last thing he remembered, anyway. Trying to put the bandanna around his thigh, and it being incredibly difficult.

When he woke, he was in Nordstrom's mercantile, laid out on a wide plank, held up by two sawhorses. And the first notion that entered his mind was that they were readying him for burial.

But then Dr. Morelli appeared at his side and said, "How do you feel, Jason?"

"Like I've been on a three-day drunk."

"That's the laudanum," Morelli replied curtly, though with a smile. "And the blood loss. That arrow you took to the leg nearly killed you. Be more careful next time, son. And now, if you'll pardon me, I have other patients. Lie still. Try to sleep."

Try to sleep? There were so many questions he wanted to ask, so many faces that he wanted to see, alive and well.

"Doc?" he asked as Morelli opened the door. "Can I see my sister? And . . . and Megan MacDonald?"

"They're toting water to the men putting out the fire at the livery. They'll be along soon enough."

Jason sighed with relief. They were both all right and unscathed if they were well enough to carry water. He fell into a deep and dreamless sleep.

When he woke again, it was night, and Jenny was sitting by his side.

"It's about time," she said, and smiled at him.

"And what time would that be?" He was feeling less well than he had before, but the wooziness was gone. Now he was sort of wishing it would came back.

"It's nine. I saved you some supper, if you're interested."

He was, and sat up to take his food. His arm was sore, but he knew it would pass. He'd checked under the bandage, and from the burns surrounding it had seen that Morelli had resorted to a little bit of old-time frontier medicine—he'd cut off most of the shaft, cut a groove in what remained, filled it with gunpowder, and shoved it out the other side of Jason's shoulder while it was burning, removing the arrow and cauterizing the wound all at once.

Smart.

He scraped the plate clean in five minutes.

"Didn't know you were that hungry, or I would have brought more," said Jenny.

"I didn't know I was that hungry, either," he said, then changed the subject abruptly. "Who lived and who died, and what happened to the rest of the Apache?"

"The Apache ran off." Jenny looked at her lap.

"Jenny?"

"Dead will be quicker."

"Thank God for that."

"Yes, I suppose so."

"Who'd we lose?"

"Gil Collins. He was dead halfway through the battle. He was dead when Dr. Morelli got to him. Elmer Jameson. He was freeing the horses from the livery when the Indians set it on fire. He never came out. Mr. Nordstrom got hit with an arrow, but he'll be all right, Dr. Morelli says. Same thing for Matt MacDonald and Ward Wanamaker."

"And that's it?"

"One of the new people, too, the ones that stayed from the last train that came through. I don't know his name, but he took an arrow to the neck and a lance to his side, and the doctor said he must have had an angel sitting on his shoulder. Both of them missed anything vital."

"The Mortons?"

"Ward and Salmon rode up to see to them. They were fine." She grinned. "I guess that when your little powder keg thing went off, Miss Europa fainted. That's what Zachary said, anyway."

"Mr. Morton," Jason corrected out of habit.

"Mr. Zachary Morton," Jenny repeated, playing along.

He paused before he said, "And Megan?"

"We've been taking turns sitting with you. She left to stretch her legs about five minutes before you woke up, you ravenous beast, you."

He grinned, then flinched.

"Lay back down. The doctor said you were to stay flat on your back for at least two days."

"Easy for him to say. He doesn't have to lie on a couple of wooden planks with no mattress and no pillow."

"Oh, don't worry. Megan's bringing quilts and a pillow from our wagon." She was talking to him like a fussy child now, and he wasn't sure he liked it.

The door opened, and instead of Megan, there stood

a contingent of townspeople, Salmon Kendall in the lead. "We've had us a meeting," Salmon said as he took off his hat. The other members of his party followed suit as they filed in.

"What sort of meeting?" Jason asked, somewhat leerily.

"Well, first off, we wanna thank you for some mighty fast thinking this afternoon. We thought you had gone off to California."

"I came back."

Salmon nodded knowingly, and so did Saul, behind him. "And why'd you do that?" Salmon went on.

"I saw the dust cloud. Didn't know if it was another marshal or Apache, but didn't figure it was worth taking the chance."

"You see?" Saul piped up. "Loyal, he is."

"And brave," added Megan, who had just stepped in, her arms full of bedding.

"Salmon, you heard me say it, Jason Fury would not let us down."

"I heard," said Salmon.

"Isn't our town named for his papa?" Saul went on. "Is not Fury a name to be reckoned with in the West?"

As a man, the crowd nodded and murmured, "Yes."

But Jason wasn't in the mood for flattery. He said, "Get to the point, Salmon."

"And he sees to the heart of the matter!" said Saul.

"The point is, Jason, we had us a little meeting. And we elected you sheriff of Fury."

"You did *what*?" Jason shouted, and was immediately sorry. His head echoed with his own words, and he put a hand to his forehead.

"For a term of two years," Saul added. "Effective immediately."

"God bless you, son," said the Reverend Milcher, who

had managed to find the farthest corner from Saul to stand in.

"I won't do it." Jason spoke more softly this time,

"I believe you will," said Saul, a half grin curving his lips.

"Why?"

"Because you can't quit 'less the mayor accepts your resignation," Wash piped up from the rear of the crowd.

"And I'm the mayor," said Salmon, leaving Jason thunderstruck.

Salmon turned to the throng and said, "I believe our own Sheriff Fury needs his rest now, folks. Shall we let him have it, or should we stay and argue some more"—he turned his head back toward Jason—"about things that can't be changed?"

The crowd began to funnel out through the door.

Jason closed his eyes in resignation and muttered, "Aw, crud."

Turn the page for an exciting preview of

BLOOD BOND:
SAN ANGELO SHOWDOWN

by William W. Johnstone
and J. A. Johnstone

BLOOD BOND:
SAN ANGELO SHOWDOWN
ISBN 0-7860-1764-3

Available August 2006

Wherever Pinnacle Books are sold

1

Dingo Whaley was the first to spot the vehicle in the distance. He had to squint a little in the bright Texas sunshine and still could not be sure if it was a wagon or carriage.

"What is it, Boss? Buffalo?"

"Shut up for a minute, Murdock, and let me think."

Pierce watched the scene from several feet away. He knew that Mel Murdock was not the brightest individual in Texas and would probably not listen to Dingo's command. Pierce didn't like Murdock—almost nobody in the gang did—so he sat back to watch the show. Murdock didn't disappoint him.

Murdock spit a stream of tobacco juice and continued. "Hell, I'm so sick of seeing the rump end of those shaggy beasts, I'd sure like to get the tail end of something a sight prettier! When are we going to hit some town—"

Without a second's hesitation, Dingo reached out and hit Murdock with a solid backhanded slap. Dingo didn't even use his full force, but it knocked the other man out of his saddle. He landed on his feet, started to reach for the gun at his side. Pierce scratched the stubble on his face, laughed softly. Murdock glanced at Pierce, then at Dingo, who was apparently ignoring him. Murdock took his hand away from the gun.

Though both men were over six feet tall and had the

well-worn look of buffalo hunters, Dingo was the bulkier of the two. He weighed in at over three hundred pounds of bone and muscle. He was said to be the best fighter and one of the fastest shots in the West. Murdock and other members of his gang knew he was also mean as sin. He was a bad man to tangle with.

"I thought I said to be quiet."

"Sure, Boss. I didn't mean to—"

"Just shut up."

Pierce laughed as Murdock got back on his horse and rode off. Pierce had no sympathy for the other man.

Dingo continued to watch the dust in the distance. He finally made out details of a single coach followed by a single rider. If it was another sodbuster, a raid would hardly be worth the effort. A more fancy rig could mean a merchant with a hidden cash box or some merchandise that could come in handy. In any case, Murdock did have a point. Dingo and his men had seen too many damned buffalo. The last big hunt had been just a few days before. It was good money—real good money. But the work was hard and tiring. Now it was time for a different kind of sport and maybe some easier money.

Another member of the gang rode up and stopped beside Pierce. He looked almost frail compared to the larger men, though he was not a small man and closer inspection revealed that he also had been hardened by years of living in the open country.

"What's cooking?" the third man asked quietly.

"Boss is in a cranky mood, Jessup. Wouldn't rile him, if I were you. Murdock made that mistake."

"Again?" He laughed. "You think he'd learn sooner or later."

"I know I don't plan on pissing off Dingo. I value my hide too much."

"Me too. Crossing Dingo Whaley is one thing nobody in their right mind would ever do."

Dingo turned his horse and rode the few feet back to the other two men.

"Jessup, you're familiar with this country. How close would you say we are to the nearest town?"

"There's a settlement or two within a half day's ride of here." Jessup absently scratched himself as he thought. "The nearest town of any size is San Angelo. Only thing much there is Fort Concho, which means you can buy beer and women."

I'm more concerned about the law."

"Hell, there may be a Ranger or two. Can't get away from those bastards these days. But the soldiers? The damned fort ain't big enough to have very many, and I'll wager most of those are new recruits who couldn't find their way home with a map. Rangers and soldiers are pretty busy with the Indians and Mexicans, anyway."

"Sounds good to me. Pierce, get the rest of the boys together. We're going to pay us a visit to those pilgrims down yonder."

Sam Two-Wolves shook his head slightly as his horse made its way through rotting corpses at the site of a recent buffalo hunt. The horse was skittish, and the smell was terrible, but Sam's firm hand kept the horse steady.

From several hundred feet away, Matt Bodine sat on his own horse. For once, he made no wisecracks, for he knew the ache that such a sight produced in Sam. He had a similar feeling in his own heart since they shared a common cultural heritage, as blood brothers. For many Indians, the buffalo was the source of life itself, and with the killing of the buffalo their life was also disappearing.

Sam was the son of a great and highly respected chief of the Cheyenne, his mother a beautiful and highly educated white woman from the East who had fallen in love with the handsome chief and married him in a Christian ceremony. As an Indian, Sam was deeply aware of the bond between men and nature, between Indian and buffalo.

Matt was the son of a rancher and met Sam when they were both just kids. The two quickly became friends, with Matt spending as much time in the Cheyenne camp as he was on the ranch at home. They grew up together, and Matt was adopted into the tribe as a True Human Being, according to Cheyenne belief. Matt and Sam were joined by a ritual of knife and fire. Though Matt's background was different than Sam's, he understood his blood brother's feelings better than most.

Their relationship was an easy one, often filled with good-natured kidding, but they could prove to be a terrible foe. On such occasions, Sam's obsidian eyes grew cold and Matt's temper could take hold. Both were young, in their mid-twenties, handsome and muscular, over six feet tall and weighing over two hundred pounds, though Sam's hair was black and Matt's was brown. They worked together individually and as a team, after having survived dozens of fights and shoot-outs in their travels across the West, in which they were now earning the reputation of gunfighters.

They came by their fighting ability honestly. Sam's father, Medicine Horse, had been killed during the Battle of the Little Big Horn after he charged Custer, alone, unarmed except for a coup stick. Realizing the inevitability of war, the chief had ordered Sam from the Indian encampment before the battle, to adopt the white man's ways and to forever forget his Cheyenne blood. That was a promise that Sam had a difficult time keeping.

Matt and Sam had witnessed the subsequent slaughter at the Little Big Horn, though that was a secret only they shared. During the time following the death of Sam's father, Sam and Matt decided to drift for a time in an effort to erase the terrible memory of the battle. Though they were often mistaken for out-of-work drifters, in truth the two men were well educated and wealthy. Sam Two-Wolves was college educated, while Matt had been educated at home by his mother, a trained schoolteacher. Sam's mother had come from a rich Eastern family and left him with many resources. Matt had earned his fortune through hard work and smart business moves. He rode shotgun for gold shipments and as an army scout, then invested his money in land. Matt and Sam now owned profitable cattle and horse ranches along the Wyoming-Montana border.

"You can't do anything about this now," Matt called out to Sam. "Let's move on."

"I know," Sam answered. "But this is such a waste. I'd like to get my hands on the men that did this."

"Yeah. So would I. But it's all legal, sanctioned and encouraged by the government."

Sam urged his horse down the road at a faster pace. He said, "Let's get out of here before I get sick."

Matt looked around, shook his head, then hurried to catch up. He would give Sam a few miles to regain his natural good humor. Sometimes it was better not to push, and this was one of those times.

Peter Easton shuffled some papers around on the makeshift desk in front of him. His ample stomach made the maneuver difficult. Carl Holz, Easton's assistant, knowing Easton's sensitivity to his weight, said nothing. The carriage shifted on the rocky ground, tossing the papers into the air. Easton tried to grab them, as did Holz.

"Damn! How's a man supposed to get any work done in these conditions!"

"I suggest again, sir, that you might be better off postponing work until you reach Fort Concho," Holz said. "All the pertinent information is in the summary I prepared for you."

Holz was much slimmer than Easton, though his hair was also slicked back and both wore expensive suits. Holz picked up a slip of paper from beneath another stack and handed it to his superior. Easton repositioned his glasses and again read through the report.

"Damn these Mexicans anyway," he said. "They can't control their own bandits and they get upset because one or two of our men cross the border in pursuit. Harumph!"

"One man in particular," Holz corrected.

"A Texas Ranger named Josiah Finch." He reached into the stack and pulled out another slip of paper, glanced down a list. "I might point out that the complaints aren't limited to just Mexican authorities. The Department has received complaints from Indian Territory, New Mexico. . . ."

"I get the idea. This Ranger doesn't understand limits—though I understand that *all* these Texans think they're too good to follow the rules. I'll conduct my investigation, make my recommendations, and get back to Washington as soon as possible." He looked out the window at the dry countryside. "I'd just as soon be back there now. Damn, I wish I had left that senator's wife alone. . . ."

A gunshot that sounded like a cannon suddenly filled the air and a hole exploded in the side of the wagon, filling the inside with splintered wood. This time the papers scattered and nobody bothered to pick them up as the horses spooked and started to run down the road. Easton and Holz hit the floor as another shot made a second hole in the side.

Outside, Dingo Whaley and his men were quickly overtaking the vehicle. The escort on horseback squeezed off a shot at the attackers, who returned the fire. A half-dozen bullets hit him at the same time and he fell to the ground. The driver, not willing to be a hero and be shot for his efforts like the escort had been, tried unsuccessfully to stop the team. Dingo solved that problem by aiming his big buffalo gun at the lead horse and squeezing off a shot. It dropped in its tracks, causing the remaining frightened horses to stumble and fall. The driver flew through the air like a rag doll. Dingo started to take aim, tracking the body as he might a flying duck, the lowered the gun and turned his attention back to the wagon.

The hitch broke and the wagon overturned in a cloud of dust and noise.

It had been many miles since Matt and Sam had left the buffalo carcasses, but Sam was still quiet.

"I could sure go for a hot meal and a cold beer," Matt said. "I'm sick and tired of this trail grub. Why, that breakfast we had this morning was—"

"You cooked breakfast," Sam answered.

"Oh. Right. Well, what about the dinner yesterday. . . ."

"You cooked dinner yesterday," Sam answered.

"Damn right! Maybe it's time you did some of the cooking!"

"What? And listen to your griping?"

But Sam smiled, and Matt grinned in return.

"That's more like it," Matt said. "You're mighty poor company when you're in one of your moods."

"*My* moods! Hell, even at my worst, I'm better than you are when you get all goggle-eyed over some saloon singer. . . ."

Matt shook his head. "Well, now I've done it! You're back to normal. Me and my big mouth! All you need now is a good fight to put you in a *really* fine mood!"

The shot of a buffalo gun roared in the distance.

"As you were saying, brother, my mood's rapidly improving!" Sam said, as he turned his horse and raced toward the sound.

Matt rolled his eyes toward the sky. "Me and my big mouth!"

2

Carl Holz touched his forehead and felt wet. He pulled back his hand and saw blood. When he volunteered to assist Easton in his department investigation, as a "favor" to an influential senator, Holz had hoped to make some points for himself to further his career. He had not planned on getting shot at. What had happened? He blinked, and found himself looking into the barrel of a Colt revolver held by one of the biggest men he had ever seen. Others had their guns pointed at Easton.

"Come on out, nice and easy," one of the men said. "I haven't decided whether or not to shoot you. If you co-operate, we might let you walk away."

Holz groaned and pulled himself out of the carriage. Easton was trying to take control, though west Texas and a gang of outlaws were much different than the Washington, D.C., society that he was familiar with. At least a dozen men, all wearing masks, held guns on them.

"Who are you? And what do you want?"

"Names aren't no matter," Dingo replied. "And what I want is your watches. Your money. Anything that you might have stashed in that fancy wagon of yours."

"Outlaws!" Holz said.

"I'll handle this," Easton hissed.

"Think you're hot stuff, do you?" another outlaw

asked. "Then handle this!" His massive fist snaked out and hit Easton, who fell backward in a daze. Easton kept his eye on him, trying to clear his head.

"Murdock, cut it out," the first outlaw said. "Pierce, you take some of the boys and take this fancy rig apart. The rest of you boys take whatever valuables you can find off these yahoos."

"Can I beat up on them some, too?" Murdock asked.

"Just do what you're told."

Holz was amazed to see Pierce and three others manually set the carriage upright again. Some of the papers that Easton had been working on fluttered to the ground through the open door.

"What's this?" Dingo demanded, kicking one of the sheets with a dirty boot. "You some kind of lawyers or something?"

"We're with the government," Easton said. He was still on the ground, rubbing his chin, trying to stand.

"Really, now." Dingo motioned to a smaller man. "Jessup, gather together some of these papers. It might prove interesting reading on some cold night." He laughed and pounded his fist on his knee.

"You can't do that! It's government property. . . ."

Murdock ripped the watch from Easton's pocket and pushed him back to the ground. He pulled his gun and aimed it at Easton's head.

"Aren't we citizens?" Jessup asked calmly.

"Ah, well . . . convicted felons do lose certain rights. . . ."

Jessup walked over and grabbed Easton's shirt collar. "What makes you think we're felons?"

"Ah, well . . ."

"Maybe you should apologize?"

"Of course. My mistake."

". . . and citizens with every right!" Holz finished.

From inside the carriage came a whoop, and one of

the men came out holding a heavy bag. It clinked as he walked.

"We struck paydirt, Boss!" the outlaw called out. "Looks like gold coin!"

Holz sighed. It had been his idea to bring along the gold to help with expenses. In the West, he knew, government IOUs weren't always considered acceptable currency. The loss of the gold could be a mark against him. Even so, he wasn't going to get himself killed over it, though he should at least make an effort.

"Anything else?" the leader of the band asked.

"You realize that this is a federal offense?" Holz asked.

"It makes me shiver in my boots!" Dingo laughed again. Holz said nothing more. "Now answer my question. Anything else of value here?"

"Nothing. You've cleaned us out."

"What about these yahoos? Should we shoot them?"

"Why waste bullets?" We're miles from anywhere. These tenderfoots won't last a day—"

Dingo stopped in mid-sentence as he seemed to listen to the air. Some said he could hear, see, and smell buffalo—and men—miles away. It made him one of the more dangerous buffalo hunters, and outlaws, working in that part of Texas.

"We're getting company," he announced. "I don't know how many, but I think we've had enough fun for one day. Let's get out of here."

Murdock laughed and added, "You're right, Dingo! Let these greenhorns stew in their own fat!"

The others also guffawed as they quickly mounted and started to ride.

Holz knew Easton was sensitive about his weight, but was still surprised to see Easton unexpectedly stand and jump at the outlaw who'd made the comment about him being fat. He grabbed the outlaw's legs and tried to drag him from the saddle. The outlaw was apparently even more surprised. He looked down at his attacker, kicked, and lost his balance. He hit the ground with a thud. The other members of the gang didn't even bother to look back as they rode away.

"Now you've done it," the outlaw said. "I've had enough. I don't care what anybody says. I'm going to kill you."

His threat was interrupted by two bullets whizzing past him. One came from behind a rock—the driver who had been hurled from the vehicle. The other shot was from a tall man riding toward him on a fast horse.

Sam Two-Wolves knew better than to rush blindly into a fight. It was better to know the odds, know who was fighting and why. But this time Sam was angry and he didn't really care. He would be willing to face a den of rattlesnakes, if need be.

That what he found was a buffalo hunter was a stroke of good fortune.

Sam instantly sized up the situation. One man with a gun, pointed at another man, ready to shoot. A third man, bloodied, apparently helpless. The wrecked carriage. The dead rider motionless on the ground. It would be unusual for one man to do so much damage, so the other gang members would probably not be too far away.

Matt also realized the situation and called out, "I'll look for the others!"

Sam waved him away and didn't slow his horse for a second. He was willing to take his chances.

He was still too far away for a clear shot, but it was worth a try. He pulled his rifle and took aim. It was almost impossible to shoot a rifle accurately from a running horse, though Sam did better than most. The shot roared almost at the same time as another, fired by a man lying behind a rock. Both shots missed. The outlaw leaped behind the cover of the damaged carriage.

Sam shot three more times, not expecting to hit his target, but giving the two other men a chance to scurry to safety behind the rock. Sam slid off his horse and joined them.

"Got yourself in some kind of mess?" he asked conversationally.

"He called me fat!" Easton said, his face red. "That was so . . . so . . . unacceptable!"

Sam raised his eyebrows.

"I'm guessing you were also robbed and your lives threatened. Was that acceptable?"

The outlaw fired two shots blindly in the direction of Sam and the others. Sam returned the fire, but continued the discussion as if he didn't have a care in the world.

"I beg your pardon. My name is Carl Holz. This is Peter Easton. We're representatives of the government, on the way to Fort Concho to conduct some business. . . ."

Easton quickly calmed down.

"Guess that was a crazy thing to do, attacking that man just because he called me a name. I could have been killed!"

"I understand. I'm kind of sensitive sometimes, myself. Problem is, I just shot the bastard. You never know."

"Are you all crazy?" the driver asked. "We've just been robbed, we're being shot at, and we're trapped! And you're all yapping your gums!"

"Not entirely correct!" Sam said. "We're not trapped at all. In fact, the fellow over there is the one in trouble. You stay here, and I'll take care of him."

Sam fired a shot and quickly reloaded. The outlaw

returned the shots. Sam zigzagged across the short distance between the rock and the overturned wagon, dodging the bullets. The outlaw fired again, but this time the hammer fell on an empty chamber. Sam covered the remaining ground in a long leap.

Matt had kept up with Sam for most of the way to the place from which the shots had come. When he also saw the damage, but only one outlaw, he changed directions at the last minute. He had a feeling that other members of the gang were near and might unexpectedly return. His guess that they were still close by was proven right when he spotted the dust cloud in the distance.

The gang was riding fast, though they did not have much of a head start. Even so, there wasn't much need for Matt to give chase. He was outnumbered and at this point had no reason to look for a fight. His intent now was to ensure that they did not turn around and surprise Sam in his skirmish with the lone bandit.

At one point the dust cloud paused, as if the gang members were considering a return, but then the group continued on its way.

"No honor among thieves," Matt said to himself.

He watched the cloud grow smaller and then disappear before turning back to join up again with Sam.

Dingo and his gang had stopped briefly to rest and water the horses by a small stream. Dingo was looking back at the trail. Pierce also looked, but could see nothing. He looked up at Dingo with narrowed eyes and asked, "Aren't we going back for Murdock?"

"No."

"Why not? There can't be that many . . ."

"There's only two. I didn't see them, but that's my guess. But somehow I sense these two are different in some way. They could mean trouble for us, and I don't intend to look for trouble before its time. I don't intend to give up what we've gained just because that fool Murdock can't stay on a horse. Of course, if you want to go back, nobody's stopping you."

Pierce shrugged, and said, "He's no friend of mine. Way I look at it, he'll get what he deserves."

"I thought not."

"What if he talks?"

"If he gets any ideas about squealing, we'll just take him out. Simple solution to the problem. No more problem."

"What's the plan now?"

"We take the money we got from the buffalo hunt and the gold that those greenhorns so kindly provided to us and have ourselves some fun. There's some whiskey and women waiting for us."

"Fort Concho?"

"That's too close—no use taking chances. Let's head south. How does old Mexico sound to you?"

Sam landed on the outlaw. The force pushed him to the ground. He punched Sam in the chest with a closed fist, but Sam was young, strong, and muscular. He shrugged off the blow and rose to his feet.

"I don't know who you are, but you've gone and tangled with the wrong guy," the outlaw said. "Nobody messes with Mel Murdock."

"Yeah, I've heard those kind of threats before."

Murdock was heavier than Sam, but he was also slower. Sam ran toward Murdock, then pivoted at the last minute.

Instead of the punch that Murdock expected, he found Sam beside him. Sam pounded the side of Murdock's head with a series of short, quick punches.

Murdock finally managed to dodge one of the blows and kick out viciously. Sam caught the foot and twisted, forcing Murdock to the ground.

In his anger, Sam was less cautious than he normally would have been. He twisted the leg until it felt as if it would give, but in a surprisingly quick move, Murdock also twisted and kicked with his other leg. This again hit Sam in the chest, but with enough force that it pushed him back. Murdock, though limping, moved in with some more blows to Sam's stomach and chest, trying to wear Sam down.

In spite of Murdock's efforts, however, Sam was not getting tired. He just kept coming back for more, handing out more punishment than he received.

Sam directed his anger at Murdock, pummeling him with a series of short, hard blows to the stomach and head. Murdock evaded some of the punches, but not enough. His face had become covered with blood.

Finally, seeing he couldn't win, Murdock pulled out a long skinning knife and rushed. Sam was no stranger to knives, however, and sidestepped, grabbed the outlaw, and threw him toward the wagon. He hit with a thud, but jumped up and ran again toward Sam.

A bullet whizzed past Sam and hit Murdock in the shoulder. He dropped his knife and fell backward against the wagon.

Leaning over the top of a rock was the driver, smoke still curling from his gun.

More Western Adventures
From Karl Lassiter

THE MOUNTAIN MAN SERIES BY
WILLIAM W. JOHNSTONE